Isabella

Crime has never looked this fabulous.

Book One in the Mated Fortune Series

J.P. Mooney

ISBN: 978-1-8380351-1-2

www.jpmooneyliterature.co.uk

DEDICATION

To Venus.

CONTENTS

ACKNOWLEDGMENTS

Thank you all for your patience.

Chapter One

Isabella

It started a year ago, Frank decided that it would be a great idea to find a source of income without being chained to a soul grinding office environment in the city. Frank is my best friend. Our friendship is solely built on bourbon, parties and shopping trips funded by rich men. We do what we want and refrain from judging each other. Yes, we have a no strings attached friendship. I am twenty-six years old. Most of the time I feel really old, like I have lived my life in my teenage years and have nothing left to look forward to. What I grew to trust throughout my days of partying is that there was no meaning to life. With this in mind, I decided to buy an apartment by the river in a beautiful city. London. My first love. Even with the constant rush of traffic, drug dealing and politics, I felt at home and secure. At least I thought I did. My name is Isabella, and this is my story.

Frank and I met at a farmers' market in Bloomsbury. We bumped into each other and he dropped my hot dog on the ground, so he insisted on buying me another one. Some would say we had an instant connection. I wondered if we could sustain a relationship though, he quickly disclosed that he was only interested in men. Regardless, I was happy to have made his acquaintance. His boyfriends were mirrored in his image, draped in the same designer rags as himself. They were oblivious about each other as he was smart enough to make sure they never found out that he was a player. I, on the other hand, didn't judge as I was engaged to my own secrets. Anyway, after we met, we started spending a lot of time together going to museums, bars, galleries that eventually led us to clubs. Frank and I never really asked each other about our past and I suppose my mouth would've never parted with the words of my truth.

We were walking down an alley in Soho one evening when we bumped into a woman wearing an attempt of a dress. Her fourth-day, wild strawberry red hair streaked with oil, her lips were stained with Malbec lipstick and her thigh-high boots grazed the crevice of her bum cheeks. She either floated on ecstasy or battled her demons with vodka so, we continued to walk while Frank switched side to be my loyal protector, in case she decided to start trouble. As we approached the road ahead our eyes attracted us to a group of men, most likely in their forties suited and handsome, each accessorised with a luxury cashmere scarf. These men were not waiting for their wives or girlfriends; they were waiting for service. I could hear the whispers amongst them as we walked past, and they eventually beckoned us over for a chat. After we chatted with the men that night, Frank convinced me that it would be a great idea to sleep with one of them. His name was Jack and he was a patron at club *MAZE*. We went back to his hotel, opened a bottle of wine and got comfortable. The entire situation was cliché and unnecessary. He just would not let the questions go, demanding information about where I grew up, and about my relationship with my father. Jack noticed I was growing impatient, so he finished his wine and got down or rather, he *went* down and dirty.

Since I journeyed on the right side of eighteen, I made affirmations to never tell anyone about my family or my life experiences. Turning my back on Dorset with my mind set on new opportunities though risky, was the best decision I made in my life. The city was my secret diary where I spilt my tears alone at night, sipped an entire bottle of Pinot Noir and anxiously waited for that dreaded knock on the door. Since my mother died, I had developed acid for plasma and a stone for a heart. The morning after I slept with Jack I woke up and found two thousand pounds on the pillow and a note, instructing that I needed to collect something from a boutique in the designer district under his name. When I arrived, the snotty saleswoman at the counter said that I needed to fit for a pair of shoes. From that day I expected nothing less from men. Most times, I enjoyed the general company of older men, whether it was an upscale dinner date at Nouveau or fully funded shopping trips in Milan with Frank. The more money I made, the better my lifestyle flourished.

Chapter Two

I woke up feeling incredibly anxious. My immediate reaction was to grab my phone from the bedside table and scroll through my recent phone calls, messages and emails however, my phone was not in its usual place. I rolled off the bed and hallucinated the furniture hanging from the ceiling mocking my pitiful wobbly legs. Since it was a Saturday, I knew that Isabella would be in the kitchen eating breakfast while nonchalantly glancing over a magazine or a shopping website. Relying on her ability to reason, I took comfort in knowing she would clarify my anxiety with answers. Shoving my lower half in a pair of silk pyjama bottoms, I made my way to the kitchen to find that Isabella was not in my apartment. My phone, however, lived. Perched on the dining table begging me to swipe. It could've been the slush of whisky and vodka I thought, when I noticed my insides pulsing non-enthusiastically while I checked through my recent call log. I called Isabella and went straight to voicemail.

"Hey, where are you? Call me back ASAP, I feel so weird after last night. Can't remember what happened."

I looked around the house and it was surprisingly clean, the perfect cover-up for a murder scene. My head started to spin alerting me to hydrate or die. My phone vibrated and I sprinted across the kitchen to answer.

"Hey! Where the fuck are you?"

"Frank, sorry I missed your call. How was your big night?"

My big night? I didn't even remember how I got home. There was a short silence on the line, and I could hear a man whisper something to Isabella.

"Oh, babes you said you were going out partying with some friends, perhaps you had one too many. Just drink loads of water and go back to bed, it's Saturday. Speak later I have to go-" The line went dead.

Isabella and I rarely partied without each other unless she had an important client. Yes, I mean international businessmen. We were walking down an alley one evening when a group of men called us over. I usually swat them away though this time they were really interested in her. She connected with one of them and they invited us to *MAZE*, an expensive members' only bullshit kind of club and she ended up going home with him. It turned out he was married with four children and lived in Italy. Since he bought her a lavish pair of designer shoes and paid for her time, she was hooked. She continued to source for new clients and made more than enough money to chase the high of her lifestyle and paid for her chic apartment on the south bank. I certainly encouraged and helped her source clients since she occasionally invited me to accompany her on shopping trips overseas while her clients conducted business. Isabella is extraordinarily gorgeous although it wasn't just her overall appearance that appeased men. Her earthy brown eyes could suck the most private person into oblivion and make them confess their secret.

I hated Monday mornings especially once the cold air had settled over the city. Typical London with shorter days and devilish longer nights. Longer nights for me meant more party invitations especially as we approached Christmas. I had been too busy working lately that I didn't have time to catch up with Isabella. I feared she was growing frustrated and upset however; I found that buying her forgiveness with some champagne and chocolates always sufficed. Most people pondered over my glamorous job but to me, it was more of a hobby I got paid to do. I absolutely loved working with people and making fabulous conversation. Five years ago, I decided I was going to be a professional Art Gallery Host. The salary wasn't enough to fund my daily cab ride home so after a year of mingling with the elite I landed a great position hosting private parties at a gallery on the river. The key to my job was knowing how to make anyone feel comfortable and at his or her best, which meant that I was a convincing liar.

Wasting my morning by lounging in bed was a choice and that choice made me late for work. I walked into my favourite Italian bakery to grab a cannolo and some tea when I bumped into an acquaintance, John who had a massive crush on his darling Isabella. All the straight men I knew fancied her, but John was different. He didn't just want to sleep with her and leave, he wanted to take her on dates and have a genuine relationship however, Isabella was not interested. He wasn't bad on the eyes though I could see why she avoided him at parties, rolled her eyes when he interrupted our weekly brunch and crossed the road when she saw him on the street. He was the type of rich man who kept to himself, carried a heavy leather bag and stared intently at you in conversations, however, I got the sense that something was not quite right. As John and I sat down, I took a second to admire the chic minimalist décor of the bakery, I did this every time I went there.

"So, Frank, how's Isabella? I hardly see you with her these days." I found the way he said her name a bit weird and irritating.

"She's great John, we've both been quite busy lately and we haven't had time to see each other much"

"What a shame, I've been quite busy myself my shares are plummeting, and It's been quite stressful, with the charity and all I've had no time for myself." He said as I noticed the bite marks that crept up his neck.

I wanted to indulge in the conversation as much as I liked having a prostate exam. Without making my boredom obvious, I finished my cannolo and excused myself. I was putting on my jacket when John whined "Tell Isabella to call me", cringing with embarrassment for the bloke, I politely nodded while making my way out of the bakery. To my satisfaction, my cab was waiting so I decided to call Isabella on the way. She picked up on two rings.

"Hello, stranger". She sounded fresh and happy.

"Someone got laid. Either that or you received my champagne and chocolates."

"Darling, I loved your gift. You really know how to make your girl happy. We need a catch-up and the quick phone call from Saturday doesn't count. Sorry about that by the way, I was with a client."

"I know, we rarely go out without each other and I got so drunk on bourbon and everything else people bought me, I almost induced myself into a coma." I laughed so loud the driver breathed a heavy sigh that prompted the rolling of my eyes.

"Well, it sounded like you had fun. How about we meet up for dinner tonight at ViV?"

"Sure, I'm late for work so I won't be done till 8 p.m. I'll be there at 8.30 p.m. I have to go, darling, bye."

I hung up the phone and walked into the gallery, headed straight to my locker, grabbed my blazer and promptly sashayed into the party, that was full of elite art buyers and their shimmering mistresses. The entire charade was pretentious, the mistresses pretended to know a thing or two about art, engaging in mundane chatter and insincere compliments to each other while the men networked and set up meetings to sign contracts. Regardless of my opinions towards these people, I was paid good money to do the job which consisted of engaging conversations until the event was over and the directors were satisfied with the profits. I grabbed a glass of champagne off the waiter's tray, worked the room by complimenting the ladies and networked with the men. The truth is I knew nothing about art, I was extremely good at talking that people would've never guessed an imposter. Once my stomach started to rumble with hunger, work was done, and I was on my way to meet Isabella when Sebastian's name vibrated on my phone screen. He was one of my friends who I occasionally invited over to the apartment for casual sex. At first, I thought it would become awkward if I bumped into my other dates in town with Sebastian on my arm, but it turned out that his job required him to travel often and we only met once every few weeks which suited me just fine. I should confirm that none of my dates had any knowledge of each other. Sebastian was a special circumstance where we had a meaningful friendship with a great understanding of each other's needs.

"Hi babe, fancy some kisses tonight?"

'Sure, I'm meeting my friend for dinner. Come by after 10.30 p.m. And I want more than just kisses."

I couldn't help but smile with excitement. I arrived at ViV and the receptionist escorted me to our table that already had a bottle of red wine and two glasses set for our enjoyment. I saw that Isabella had already started sipping and therefore, already working up an appetite for dinner which was just as well since I was now on the verge of starving. Isabella looked gorgeous in her black pencil dress and her hair was silky straight although she knew I preferred her sassy curls.

"Look at you handsome." She beamed.

"I see Pilates have been doing you well."

I sat down and gave her a kiss on the cheek. The waitress came straight over and set down a platter of appetizers. I loved that she prepared for my arrival, I was always either starving or in need of a tipple.

"I have missed you, Frank, tell me everything."

We divulged in general conversation. I told her about the party I went to and my relations with Sebastian which had developed over a few months and that he had slept over almost every night in the last three weeks. I also brought up John and she cringed at the mention of his name. We ate, drank our wine and she told me about her clients and her annoying partner at Pilates whom, she was trying to tolerate as she refused to find another studio just because someone tried to make her one hour of mindfulness unbearable. I kissed her goodnight and told her I would call in the morning.

◈

Isabella

In the taxi home, I simmered in tranquillity after seeing Frank. I couldn't stop thinking about the bore of my life, John who kept asking Frank about me. Part of me wanted to give him a chance since he was wealthy, and I liked nice things yet, the other part of me was afraid of his judgements once he found out what I did for money. I had no reason to be afraid since we were cordial from afar and he was irrelevant to my life although my past experience had taught me to be vigilant and trust my instincts. Despite his charming smile and over the top polite quirks, something was not quite right with his energy. I noticed my phone had a voicemail from an unknown number.

"Hello Isabella, it's John. (Did I also mention how much I hated the way he said my name?) Listen, I got your number from Frank. I would like to know if you would accompany me for dinner at ViV Tomorrow. Call me back." I couldn't believe Frank gave him my number. My heart started to race, and a nervousness unsettled me. I decided to call Frank.

"Hello." He sounded busy.

"You little prick! Why would you give John my number before asking me?" I said pacing back and forth.

"Well, darling if I asked you first you would've said no." I could feel his smirk.

"Bloody right I would've said no!" The audacity of this man.

"Seriously calm down, give the man a chance. He's rich and to be honest I couldn't not give it to him. As a man, I felt sorry for him because he genuinely likes you." I imagined Frank sitting on his bed or sofa, all giddy and smirky while Sebastian caressed his chest.

"Whatever." And with that, I hung up and headed to the shower.

I came out of the shower and poured some crisps in a bowl accompanied by a bourbon. Telling myself not to return the call didn't quite work since I was lured into everything my mind protested against, like telling a child not to press a button knowing that the idea of being told not to do it would indeed result in the opposite action. I decided to call him.

"Hello." Shit, I was nervous.

"Hi John, it's Isabella I just got your voicemail. How are you?" I said while staring at myself in the hallway mirror.

"Oh, what a pleasant surprise." I also wasn't keen on his phone voice but that was something I pushed to the side for the meantime.

"Erm, I'll have dinner with you."

"Wow great, I'll pick you up tomorrow at 7 p.m. See you then."

And just like that, I had a date with John. Why did I agree to this? The answer to this question was non-existent but, I was mildly happy with my decision. It was also scary since I had always kept a close eye on everyone I allowed to walk in and out of my life, scrutinising every detail and ensuring that they weren't a threat to my life and my money. This scrutiny also applied to Frank. Since it was a lovely calm evening, I decided to relax on the balcony overlooking the sparkly stars of the city.

Chapter Three

While Sebastian and I enjoyed a glass of Barolo my phone rang and obviously, it was Isabella. I knew exactly why she was calling. I had known her long enough to comprehend when she had made naughty decisions, going against everything she protested not to do.

"Well that didn't take long darling," I said with a smirk.

"I said yes, that I'll go on a date with him." There was a short silence.

"Well, that's great, what changed your mind?" I was genuinely curious.

"Besides the fact that I couldn't be rude and reject him? Well, he seemed like a nice person and I would never turn down a free dinner."

Even though she tried to humour the situation, I knew that there was a chance she was interested in going out with John because she possibly entertained the idea of fondness for him. Isabella was a peculiar flower with secrets I was afraid to ask her about yet, it was no secret that she had special interests in older men. I guessed that perhaps it was an opportunity for her to learn and develop herself from someone who had already walked the path. Besides, older men were nurturing in a fashion that most men our age couldn't be. As soon as I got off the phone, Sebastian pinned me against the wall and kissed me.

I woke up naked as Sebastian emerged from the kitchen with a cup of coffee. He was even more gorgeous without the hair gel and I really liked him. Surely, he felt the same, I just couldn't allow myself to fall in too deep since he travelled a lot and I certainly didn't want to tie myself down with emotional attachment that could all end in messy tears. Many years ago, I made a conscious choice to never permanently give myself to anyone, which is why I only saw Sebastian when necessary and the same applied to my other dates. Moreover, tying myself down mentally and emotionally meant that I couldn't sleep with other men and that's an idea that made me shudder.

"What are you thinking about?" Sebastian asked with a grin. The type of grin that made me want to get on my knees.

"Nothing." I also hated the small talk which meant taking responsibility for bonding and expressing feelings for each. It was tedious. We finished our coffee and I sent Sebastian on his way.

"So, what do you plan on wearing?" I said while sitting on Isabella's bed nibbling some of her homemade brownies. She picked out a dark green pencil dress from her clothing rack and put it on.

"Is this too formal? I don't want to look like his assistant." We both laughed.

"You look gorgeous regardless. So why did you agree to this then, really?" She ceased doing her makeup for a moment and looked at me, her eyes piercing through my soul. God, she was beautiful.

"I don't know Frank. All he does is ask about me. Maybe I just need to give him a chance, worst-case scenario, we could be friends." Ouch. She had already thought of placing him in the friend zone. She proceeded to do her makeup. I couldn't fault her for being honest.

"How do I look?" She said with a devilish smile.

"Beautiful!" We hugged and John picked her up. I made my way home and decided to call Sebastian over for the night.

Isabella

We arrived at ViV and John held the door open for me. I knew he wanted me to walk in front of him so that he could stare at the back of my dress. I caught myself and became aware of my criticism then remembered that since this man had pursued me for a long time, I should keep my cool. We sat in a corner booth and I noticed how good he smelled. My nose naturally reacted to the hint of woody musk nonetheless, I couldn't put my finger on the note, I just knew that it was something classic and I was impressed.

"So, Isabella thank you for accepting my dinner invitation." He said with the sincerest smile.

"It's no problem." I mean what else could I say.

We ordered our food and some wine. John didn't talk much about his work which was fine with me as I was reluctant to disclose information about mine. I did learn that he enjoyed dancing which was a passion of mine and possibly the foundation for a hot sex life. He started to grow on me.

"You seem a little distant, is something wrong?" His soothing voice snapped me back to reality.

"No, sorry I'm just a little bit tired. I had a late night." I lied.

"That's quite alright, do you want to leave?" He said with detachment.

"Not at all." We stared at each other for a moment and despite what I'd heard happened on dates, my stomach didn't flip with butterflies.

We talked about several of our interests although I didn't tell him what I did for a living nor did he question when I said I was a blogger which is what I told people when I didn't want to exhibit the truth about how I afforded a chic apartment on the south bank. John was charming, not bad to look at and it made me wonder that maybe I should've given him a chance in the first place. Just when I tried convincing myself that I wasn't attracted to him, he leaned over grabbed my face with both hands and kissed me. His lips were soft, and his mouth was warm, pulling me into his enchantment leaving me wanting more. We kissed for a very long time before he paid the bill and we headed home. Nothing was said about the kiss while John walked me to the door. Just when I thought I made a mistake he asked if he could come inside to have a drink.

◇

Frank

I had the day off work, so I decided to spend some time with Isabella. We parked ourselves in a cute little nail salon for a Mani-Pedi in King's Cross. She was looking stunning as usual wearing casual skinny jeans and showcased her cleavage in a fitted shirt. I knew her date with John went well because she was glowing and couldn't stop smiling.

"So, tell me all about last night." I said while blowing on my manicured fingers.

"Well…it went well I think, just don't think he's all that interesting." She glued her eyes to the floor.

"What do you mean? Didn't you invite him back to your apartment?" I knew she did because she texted me after he had left. Surely one does not invite dates back home if they didn't want it leading to something.

"Yes, but nothing happened. After our drink, I told him I was tired, so I just kicked him out." Her eyes echoed the inconvenience of the situation.

We continued to chat about life and work in general. She seemed genuinely tired however; I was dying to go out on the town.

"I hope you're not too tired. We are going out tomorrow night." I tried my best to get her on the energy train.

I received a distant "Sure." Our nails looked wonderful and I felt fresh. I pledged that it was time to get my best friend back on the scene even if it meant I had to pay for her drinks all night.

Isabella

Even though Frank tried to get me back on my devilish routine, something inside of me knew that a break from city life was very much needed. Since my date with John was cut short, I had attempted to live my life in silence. This meant avoiding John and keeping communication with Frank to a minimum as he had become needy and overindulgent since Sebastian's departure. I cared about Frank though I didn't quite care for his constant whining and pouting. During my time alone, I worked out in the park, read my books and continued to date my clients. To be honest, there were only two men. Regardless, I made enough money to buy more stocks and diversify my portfolio. Nevertheless, this bid to keep things low key was not entirely working because every time I paused to make a cup of tea, to be alone with my thoughts or even to cultivate my energy into something creative, I had mini flashbacks of my life in Dorset, the woman from Pilates and the others I would probably hurt in the future. As I sat in my custom-made chair one evening, I heard the distinctive sound of my ringtone coming from the kitchen. I knew it was a phone call from Frank, so I didn't hurry to answer. To my surprise it was John. It had been nearly two weeks since our date and I knew that I wanted nothing more to do with him. I had ignored his messages and filtered his call to voicemail a few times, so I wondered why he didn't understand that I wasn't into him.

"Hello" I muttered dismissively.

"Hi Isabella, err it's John."

"John hi, how are you?" If he didn't know I was avoiding him, he sure knew it now by the tone of my greeting.

He rattled on about how busy he had been, why he would like to meet up again and maybe this time he would cook me dinner at his house. I chuckled to myself as I knew what 'cooking dinner at his place' meant. I applauded John though. He knew what he wanted and wasn't afraid to fight for it even though his approach was pathetic. If it was someone else with spunk, I supposed it would've turned me on. We decided that we would confirm dates for dinner in the upcoming week. The date never happened, I switched my phone off during the week and avoided going to places I knew there was a chance I would bump into him. As much as I liked to dine with wealthy men, I decided that I liked to lounge in my satin pyjamas and relax on my faux fur throw more.

Chapter Four

Isabella

On a Tuesday evening, I decided to pour myself a glass of wine and plot my cheeks on the sofa. There was nothing particularly exciting on TV, so I decided to browse the Internet, maybe even treat myself to something nice. I felt restless, so I decided to walk to the shop. The sky had sliced open with rain and my skin prickled as the icy air hacked into my pores. As I walked into the shop, I noticed a man staring at a box in the cereal aisle, a light glowed around him as he scrutinised the nutritional information of the box. The muscles on his thighs were so big it stretched his skinny jeans, he enticed me and the bulging veins on his neck pulled me into a trance, beckoning me to touch them. He most definitely took care of himself. He didn't notice me and my frozen stare, so I decided to discreetly follow him around the shop. I picked up a bag of crisps, a chocolate bar and a smoothie. As I stood in the queue, I saw him grin at the sexy cashier who shamelessly fawned over him.

"As I was telling you, Andrew, their clothes will look great on you". His name was Andrew, nice.

"Fine, fine okay just tell Dave I'll give him a call". I simmered in glee as I sensed his impatience and desperate attempt to leave the shop.

I quickly paid for my things and leapt towards him to say hello. To my embarrassment, I twisted my ankle and fell right by his feet prompting him to halt.

"Oh my god, are you okay? Let me help you" I nearly fainted as he stretched his arm to check my ankle.

"I don't think I can walk" I exaggerated. He rubbed his head for a moment then balanced half of my weight on his shoulder.

"I'll walk you home and we can assess your ankle out of the rain." I should have said no but I was too far into the game to remember my protocols. Besides, I knew how to look after myself.

We walked to my building and luckily my apartment was on the second floor, I didn't have to be stuck in the lift with a hot stranger for too long. His face looked surprised as we approached the building.

"No way, you live in the same building as me?" He bemused.

"Really? I've been here just over two years and I've never seen you around". How did I not notice this man in my building?

"Yeah I live on the fifth floor and I'm a workaholic, in the office and at the gym" I'm sure I saw his chest expand under his jumper.

While Andrew watched me fiddle my key through the door lock, I realised that I had left all of my things lying on the floor including the laptop and its inappropriate browser history, my journal and incense holders. As he helped me shuffle into the apartment, I knew he was impressed with my immaculate interior. His eyes sparkled with pleasure and my face beamed with pride. We slowly shuffled to the sofa and he immediately enquired for my first aid cabinet.

"In the bathroom, second door on the left." I took his swift absence as an opportunity to shut my laptop and hide my journal behind the cushions.

"Right, let me have a look. It doesn't look broken, just a small graze. Keep it elevated and leave the ice pack on for a few minutes at a time"

"Thank you, let me buy you a drink?" Time stopped for a moment when I thought he would leap at the opportunity, though he hesitated.

"You're welcome, but I don't drink with random injured strangers off the street" Ouch. He was in my apartment and on that basis alone I didn't think of us as strangers anymore and besides, any man would be happy to have a woman like me buy them a drink.

Realising it had been over twenty seconds since he replied; I pulled myself together and displayed a polite nod. I thanked him again for his help and as the door shut behind him, I gracefully walked to the kitchen, drained my glass of wine and swallowed a prescription strength painkiller. Thirty minutes later I ascended into euphoria and decided to check who my neighbour really was. He didn't have social media accounts, nor did he have any work-related publications. It started to dawn on me, that Andrew could be off the grid just like me. As I continued to dig deeper, contemplating showing up at his door with nothing but a trench coat, my phone rang, and Frank's solemn face buzzed me out of my high.

"You're getting high without me?" This is why I loved Frank, he never judged. I briefly explained the situation with my sort of new neighbour and asked him if he wanted to come over.

"Sorry Izzy, I'm so tired and it's pissing rain outside. Maybe tomorrow."

And with that, we bid our goodnights. I decided to peel myself off the rug and indulged in a soothing long rose and cassis scented shower. My mind was in the ceiling while the wine and codeine circulated through my system. I took pleasure in drying my skin and applied some scented body lotion. I fluffed my curls loose and walked to my wardrobe, which was filled with silhouetted dresses, lace underwear and pointed-toe pumps. I slid into one of each, choosing black as my power colour and made my way to the door. I decided that for as long as I was inebriated, I deserved to have some fun. The lift crawled from my apartment to the fifth floor making me silently regret going through efforts for a stranger. I decided to go back downstairs, however, as I reached to press the button the door opened, and Andrew walked in, surprised. He was wearing a fitted cotton shirt and slim-fit black chinos. The air in the lift thickened as the particles of our fragrances waltz together. Andrew looked uncertain and I wasn't sure whether I should've been ecstatic that he saw me or embarrassed.

"What have we here?" He made a point to stare at my body. "Are you lost?" I rarely got embarrassed however, at this point I wished the lift would drop all the way to the basement and beyond.

"Erm hi, no not lost I thought I'd have a look at the building. I realised that I had never been past the second floor. The carpet here looks nicer." I was nauseated by the pitiful lie. There were a million and more excuses I could have used. He saw right through the lie and at this point I decided not to care.

"I thought I would see where my medic lived," I said with confidence.

"Okay, well I was on my way to the pub but since you're here and dressed quite nicely, how about you come in for a drink?" I was confused. He said he didn't drink with strangers, yet he invited me inside for a drink.

I reluctantly agreed and as we made our way through the corridor, I urged myself to keep my shit together. When he opened the door to his apartment my jaw dropped in delight. I was very proud of my own interior design skills however, Andrew's was magnificent. His scheme of navy-blue walls with grey furniture was not what I expected a man of his stature to execute so effortlessly. The furniture was tucked nicely in their places and the detailed accessories fitted in efficiently. The apartment was also clean and tidy. Like myself, he was proud of his not so humble abode. We made our way to the kitchen where he had a small built-in wine cooler. I immediately felt jealous for not thinking of this investment.

"Rosé?" I thought that maybe I should make up an excuse and ask for some water instead although I really wanted to ride the high, I was already on. I favoured for sipping slowly. We took our drinks to the living room and I parked myself on the rug. He hesitated for a moment then joined me. We sipped slowly or as slowly as I could without missing a breath and passing out. My ears were ringing, and my heart was beating in my throat. At that moment, I knew I wanted something outrageous to happen.

"Why are you here Isabella?" A frisson swept over me and it took me a second to realise what had just happened. How did this man know my name? He quickly answered as though he read my mind.

"Since I met you, I decided to do a little digging. I asked the concierge about you and he said all he knew was your name, Isabella. A very pretty name for a beautiful woman."

I didn't know whether to relax or stay on guard. If Andrew had been interested enough to ask about me, it meant he wanted more. More of what? That, I didn't know. For saving time's sake I thought that perhaps he wanted to make sure he knew the person he wanted to get involved with. Yes, I was tripping. Either way, I stayed quiet and tried to keep my cool. Under the codeine and wine fog, I could feel my insides slushing with adrenaline and I didn't care that he was still a stranger. After all, I had already decided to drink with him in his house and considering my earlier statement once in the house, we weren't strangers. I moved closer to him and set both our glasses on the coffee table. I unzipped my dress revealing my lace underwear as his eyes sparkled with lust and desire. I crawled to him and traced my tongue from his collarbone to his ear and bit it softly. The silence engulfed us. I unbuttoned his shirt and kissed his chest while he aimed to unhook my bra. He wrapped my legs around his waist and carried me to the sofa. My mind was reaching the clouds and my body arched to the ceiling. The fog had lifted leaving behind clarity and desire. I needed him to float with me. His lips traced every inch of my body as his hands created poetry between my thighs. He slowly entered me as our eyes connected and the energy spiked and propelled us out into space. I wanted the high to last forever and so did he. We bit and teased each other, fingers entwined like mating serpents. We were pressed into each other's bodies for what felt like a lifetime before we both came and were soaked in each other's sweat.

Thirty minutes later I sat on the rug admiring every visible detail of Andrew's apartment. Since I discreetly slipped a pill in his drink when he was in the bathroom, he had fallen asleep with ease and that bought me about an hour to browse. I was concerned that he had asked people about me so I thought I would return the favour by looking through his things for my own assurance. I had a twitch that Andrew was up to something or at least I knew not to trust him. I made my way to his bathroom and opened the cabinet above the sink. The best way to find anything worth knowing about a man is to see what medicine he was taking. I caught a glimpse of myself in the mirror, mascara and lipstick smeared into a mush across my face. I closed the cabinet and made my way to his bedroom glaring at his silk sheets, taunting me to plunge onto the bed. I opened his wardrobe expecting to find chaos. I was surprised to find his shirts hung tidily and his trousers compactly folded on their designated shelves. Fifteen minutes had passed, and I found nothing.

Growing familiar with the apartment, I strutted to the kitchen to check the cleanliness of his utensils. Upon opening the top drawer, a small notebook fell on the floor. At first, I assumed it fell from the countertop or from the inside of the drawer, perhaps a manual, however, I remembered it wasn't there when Andrew poured the wine earlier, which meant that it fell from underneath the drawer. I opened the small booklet and scanned the handwriting; names of women and a tick next to them glared back at me. I was confused. Andrew's stirring and heavy breathing startled me. I froze waiting to get caught but then I recalled the pill was wearing off. Walking to the living room, a brisk breeze stabbed through my skin reminding me to put my dress back on. As I shimmied into the dress my mind was occupied with the notebook. I checked Andrew's breathing and lightly stroked his hair reassuring myself that he would be fine. I grabbed the rest of my things, shoved the book in my bag and slipped into the corridor optimistic that nobody noticed me. Once I had showered, eaten and cocooned to the cosiness of my bedroom I started to study the pages of the notebook until sleep consumed me.

The morning was surprisingly bright and the drilling in my head was unpleasant. I crawled out of bed to grab my phone that had five missed calls from Frank, and one missed call from an unknown number. I chuckled to myself as I remembered my crazy night with Andrew. I slowly sipped my tea and glared into the distance. Once my mind had descended back to reality, I called Frank to arrange a meeting for lunch.

"Do you remember anything about last night or was it that good?" He said after the second ring.

"I do actually, and it was bloody great. I really want to have a catch up so let's meet up for lunch?" I bit my lip.

"Sure, let's meet at the Italian café around the corner from yours." I was excited yet nervous to tell Frank about my evening. Frank never judged but he did get exceptionally jealous.

I swayed to the bathroom and indulged in the cool stream of the shower, lathering my sins away. I decided to dress down with nude makeup, textured leggings and a jumper. Since the sun was out, I opted to walk off my hangover and absorb my surrounding.

Chapter Five

I was exhilarated to hear all about Isabella's shenanigans over lunch although I had a pang of jealousy that I wasn't there to experience the high with her. I spent all evening with Christian whom I rarely saw following his move to Scotland when Isabella picked up the phone, I knew she was intoxicated. There was something in her eyes, that screamed rage and it looped me into uncertainty. It projected itself effortlessly when she was under the influence and it was painful to try and comprehend. Today, even with a hangover, her eyes were luminous. I trusted that she could handle herself in any situation however, I couldn't help but raise an eyebrow about her not so new neighbour.

"I'm telling you, Frank, it was thrilling and he's so hot!" She said mid sip.

"I don't care if he's hot. Don't you think it's weird that he had a notebook full of women's names? What if he's a serial killer or a sex trafficker?" I caught myself shouting sex trafficker a little too loud. She closed her eyes and breathed in the coffee fumes.

"If he is up to something, I don't think it's that bad. Also, I'm excited to find out what it is." She gave me a cunning smile.

Something deep in my gut knew that whatever idea she had in her mind was bad. People who intruded on other people's privacy usually ended up in ditches or if they were lucky, a makeshift grave. That's what usually happened to people who refused to mind their own business. Which is why I minded my mine when it came to our friendship. I knew that there were things she never wanted me to know, things that could change our friendship albeit this mystery that she wanted to engage in, was a prime example of when someone needed to mind one's business. It wasn't long before I received a text from Christian summoning me to play. As much as I wanted to lecture my best friend about her dangerous liaisons, I decided that she was a grown-up and responsible for her own decisions. Besides, I was always the first one to jump to conclusion and for all I knew, Andrew's biggest secret could be that he was a billionaire who generously donated to the local animal shelter. I ordered myself a coffee to take away and said goodbye to Isabella who insisted on staying for another cup. On my way home, the sky opened, and drizzles of rain glistened my hair. I picked up my pace while debating on requesting a taxi. Just as I lifted my arm to get the chap's attention, I heard a 'hello' in a too familiar voice that made my skin ripple. I could feel his hopes tainted with a hint of desperation. John. Hearing his voice raised a biochemical alarm that caught me off guard. I had nothing against John however; his persistent whining about Isabella lately had dug a dent under my skin.

"Hello Frank, I thought that was you." He approached closer.

"Hi John, how have you been? I heard the big date went well" Although, I knew it was a mixed review.

"About that, I haven't heard from Isabella lately well, since our date and I was wondering if she's okay? She didn't return my calls and well, it'll be nice to see her again." This was painfully escalating into a self-indulgent pity party and I had an aggressive need to tell John that his darling Isabella was just not interested in him.

"Actually, I haven't but I'll ask her to call you." I lied while he advanced closer.

Fortunately, a taxi stopped and prevented him from invading my personal space. To my contentment we didn't have an opportunity to say goodbye nor did I want to welcome such an opportunity. As I looked in the rear window of the car, I imagined John pouring his sorrows in a tumbler of whisky at Isabella's expense. It was sad to envision indeed.

Isabella

I hadn't decided how to approach the Andrew mystery, nor did I have the slightest idea of how to proceed with the notebook. I could've given it back to him perhaps slip it under the door, but I wasn't stupid to have him on my tail and interrogate me about why I had it in the first place. The logical side of my brain wondered if he noticed the book was missing and whether he knew I stole it. The irrational side however, wondered if he even remembered last night and how exhilarated it was. With my head becoming a little clearer I slipped into my workout kit, laced up my trainers and headed for the park. I wanted to get a head start on the stairs since I lived on the second floor but surrendered to the lift. Just as the doors slid open, I saw Andrew engrossed in his phone screen. I thought we would descend without acknowledging each other's presence but then I remembered how gorgeous he was and decided to mutter a modest 'Hello'. It could have been confusion or embarrassment, though I hoped it was a look of pleasure when his eyes grew wide as he focused on my face. To my disappointment, the infinite lift journey ended without small talk or acknowledgement of the night before. While my ego wanted to sulk from his dismissive attitude, my sanity prodded me towards the park, which is where I spent my energy for the next hour.

I inadvertently walked in and out of my building that day and it was apparent that Andrew had a day off or like myself, was self-employed. Although I didn't recall him confirming the latter from our conversations. Each time the lift door opened I secretly hoped he would appear. I eventually gave up and comprehended that for once, I had sex with a man who didn't hand me an envelope full of cash, a gift or a cheque. Alarmed by this realisation, I decided to book a client to remedy my bank account. As I went about my daily routine, I found myself including casually staring outside the window into my rituals. I was amazed that it only took me a few days to learn about my neighbours' routine, including Andrew's. I saw that he left early for work, so I decided that synchronising my daily paper run with his exit would satisfy my creeping obsession. Every time we bumped into each other we muttered good morning and commented on the weather. Depending on his mood…or mine, we smiled. Most times it was often me doing the smiling. I never considered myself to fawn over men but there was something about Andrew, aside from the notebook mystery that attracted me to him. It wasn't until a week had passed that I realised it was because he was playing hard to get. Through this realisation, I decided to hold the ball in my court and withdrew myself from the situation.

Before I knew it Saturday arrived, and I was yearning for some excitement that didn't include consuming illegal drugs. I had called Frank to arrange dinner however, he was tied up with a work event. This further fuelled my frantic need to ride unicorns, so I decided to calm myself with rum and streamed a random series. As the smooth glistening liquid burned and glided down my throat prickling my intestine, I felt my body relax and the humour that spat from the TV screen consumed me. Halfway through the episode, I lost all sense of the chaotic world outside. I breathed in the scent of my apartment, a proud extension of myself. I felt secure. As I took another sip of rum, a subtle knock wafted through the creases of my door. I froze, wondering if I had offended the neighbours with the sound of my adult cartoon. Another knock, yet this time more aggressive. I peeked through the peephole and saw Andrew's face distorted by the lens. Pretending to be confused, I opened the door with the most nonchalant smile I could afford.

"Oh hello." I knew this would happen.

"Hi, I haven't seen you all week. Just thought I'll check if you're okay." He was coming to his senses.

"Yeah, I'm fine, I've been busy." We danced around the beat of silence for a moment.

"I don't want to be a dick but I'm a little preoccupied right now."

"Are you with someone? I'm sorry for interrupting I just wanted to check if your ankle was okay."

"No, I don't have company but I'm watching something. Would you like to join me?" Just like that, he fell into my trap.

I escorted him to the living room, and I saw how surprised he was to see me drinking rum. I poured him some with two ice cubes as he asked and retreated to my cosy blanket on the far end of the sofa. At the end of the episode, I knew Andrew wanted to talk so I deliberately flicked through a magazine from the coffee table and waited for him to mutter the first words.

"So, what have you been up to?"

"Working. Yourself?"

"Same. I've been meaning to catch you after work, but I've been tired and every time we bumped into each other I was grumpy. Sorry if I seemed standoffish." I gave him a polite nod although the words tracking around in my head were more insane than polite.

"So, the other night was weird. I mean it wasn't bad weird, it was just different." I frowned at him until he realised how 'weird' his comments were lapping on my ears.

"I'm sorry I don't mean weird in a bad way, it's just that I've never quite done it like that before." I was not falling for the game and my defensiveness crept in because I knew he was lying. I quickly realised that I was jealous of him being with someone else. Jealousy was the least I wanted to feel, it blinded logic and threw its victims off track.

I snapped myself out of the obscure thought and took a long sip of my drink, his action mimicked mine. We sat in silence for a moment to enjoy the atmosphere while the rum glazed our moods. I sensed a change in the air, possibly from the heat radiating from Andrew's arms or from my mind collapsing into a rum haze. Andrew's thoughts synchronised with mine and without prompt he shuffled closer to my leg, his finger lightly traced a path to my thigh. He leaned into my neck and traced his breath underneath my jaw sending a chill along my spine.

"I know all about you, you whore."

It took a while for of his words to resonate. I dropped my guard for one moment and in doing so I allowed a man to out me. My emotions went into fight or flight and since we were in my apartment, the only thing I could do was ask him to leave however, I was intrigued. I wanted to know exactly what he thought he knew about me. Retracting my face from his, I grimaced my confusion. Then I realised that he was definitely pissed off that I drugged him.

"What, don't you remember darling Isabella?" Of course, I remembered.

"I have no idea what-

Before I could finish my sentence, he stood up and walked to the corner of the room to observe the shapes protruding on each shelf of the bookcase. Although my mind was cloudy with mild confusion, (I didn't think that knowing I was an escort would conjure such over the top reaction but then again, it's not everyone's cup of tea.) The haze had cleared. The only moisture on my body was the microscopic droplets of sweat exiting the pores on my forehead. I then saw that the ice bucket was empty, so I walked to the kitchen to fetch some more. If we were going to do this, we needed more drinks. When I returned, he was still standing there.

"You have curated so many beautiful items. When I saw your apartment, I was excited because like myself you have exquisite taste. And I have the same exquisite taste in women such as yourself. When I saw you the other night, I couldn't believe my chance but then the next morning I didn't feel quite myself. It took a while for my memory to come back to me and when it did, I realised that you slipped something in my drink. To me, that was cheating and unfair. So, I want to know what kind of game you would like us to play?".

Stunned was the likely word I would use to describe my reaction, however, more so on the switch up of the game. Firstly, I didn't expect pretty boy to have a brain and secondly, I didn't expect him to notice that I had spiked his drink. In fairness, I thought he would put the fuzzy head down to overindulging on wine. Afterall, it was an exquisite rosé. I wanted to pursue the innocent game however, I knew it was best to ask him to leave before things turned ugly.

"Okay, I may or may not have put something in your drink. You're alive, aren't you? I don't really know what game you're talking about playing. Please leave."

"Ah okay, so it's like that. I don't think you realise that spiking someone's drink is actually a crime." I rolled my eyes.

He walked over and launched himself on the edge of the sofa. His body softened and for a moment I thought it was over, so we could both laugh it off. But then there was a weird shift in his eyes.

"Did you also know that tax evasion and participating in money laundering is illegal?" I really wanted to hit him with something sharp and heavy. Mostly to neutralise his ego and to punish him for poking his nose in my business.

"Now you're just being ridiculous."

"I don't think so. I had a sense that you'd been keeping an eye on me since that night for whatever reason. But then I asked myself how a beautiful woman with expensive taste afforded to maintain her lifestyle without a job?"

"How do you know I don't have a job?" I smiled.

"You should really tell your visitors to be more discreet when they're ringing your doorbell. Perhaps ensuring they ring the right door number for a start."

As much as I had wanted to indulge him in the rest of the game, I wished that Andrew would leave. Every syllable of a word his mouth formed caused rage to pour from that place I strived my entire adult life to forget. I rationalised my options and was immediately disappointed to remember that I hadn't messaged Frank in a while. The insane part of me wanted to stab him in the neck. I had to remain calm.

"Fine, okay let's assume I have sex for money and maybe I don't pay as much tax as I should, you have no proof. In fact, if you felt the need to check I can reassure you that I'm a blogger with a large social media following." I slowed my breath to steady my heartbeat.

"It's a good cover for your real job. Are you registered as self-employed? Or perhaps you provide a discounted service for clients who provided professional advice on avoiding the taxman with ghost accounts. Have a look at this."

Andrew threw his phone across the sofa and all the efforts to keep my heart from beating out of my throat were hopeless. He had a video of me with one of my clients, in conversation and all. I really wanted to ask how he managed this however, from my experience I knew that some questions were better left alone. I contemplated smashing the phone or flushing it under water though I knew that he likely had another copy of it at home. One thing I was sure on was that he couldn't have done this alone. He poured himself another rum with three ice cubes and I sat clenching my tumbler while I mapped a way out in my head. Andrew seemed content with the silence. The ice was now melted so he knocked his drink back in one and poured another with two more ice cubes. He politely excused himself and went to the bathroom. My body remained frozen even when I heard the toilet flush and the stream of water in the sink. I heard his slow footsteps in the corridor as he eventually staggered and slumped on the sofa. His eyes slowly closed as the muscles on his body released him into a limp dreamy state. I placed my drink on the coffee table and bit my lip as I gazed over him. I knew how to look after myself and there was no way he was leaving without reversing the situation. The ice cubes were laced with Vicodin. I checked the time and steadied my breath. If I wanted to know the who, what's and why's I had to get a move on the situation.

Sixteen years old, and all I wanted to do was go to arcades with my friends, read books and pass my exams. I looked forward to the world and I had every bit of my expectations invested in the hope that the world would accept me. Curly hair, brown eyes and earth brown skin. The moment I enrolled in college the bubble of expectations disappeared and I had my first experience of how hellish this world really was. Everyone hated me because I was different. My parents were financially comfortable. My mum taught me that to be taken seriously, I needed armour and the only way we knew how, was to straighten our hair and regularly exfoliate our skin. I soon ditched the books, failed my exams and founded a killer pout. However, I wasn't foolish. In the age where every selfie descended on social media sites within a millisecond; I kept a low profile and avoided people who had special interest in my personal life.

On the edge of seventeen, my dad died in a car accident. The hell that I knew when I started college was nothing compared to the hell that swallowed my mother shortly after he died. My father's death presented us with a deep hole in the family's name. A debt that forced us to downsize into an apartment where I witnessed my mother numb her pain with vodka. She tried to keep up with the flash image hosting regular afternoon soirees and recycling pre-loved designer items, but eventually, she was forced to sell her jewellery and accepted that the life she knew was now very much over. Then, she met Paul. There was a special place below where people like Paul ended up. He was the type of man who thought it was acceptable to beat women. I dreaded the nights he slept over. I knew that once he thought I had tucked myself into bed, he would pick a fight with my mother.

One evening, I decided to fake a cold to skip awkward tension over dinner. I left the bedroom door ajar with my head pressed firmly against the pillow and a baseball bat rested in the grip of my hand under the duvet. Everything in my bedroom lacked life and personality except the glare that sliced through the door. I heard Paul mumble as he smoked a joint and my mother, who was pouring her evening ritual into her favourite glass. Paul was not a fan of this act which was one of the reasons why he felt the need to 'correct' her. Usually, there were build-ups to the physical commotion, my heart leaped when I heard the bottle shatter on the floor. A silent panic surged through me as I indirectly felt the pinch of friction that struck my mother's face. I closed my eyes, breathed deeply and slowly counted down from ten. With the bat held taut in my hand I climbed off the bed and headed for the door. As I approached the living room, Paul's hands were firmly wrapped around my mother's throat like a snake enveloped around its game. Her voice was raspy as she gasped for air.

Five...four...each step was singed with fury. Three... two...I swung the bat with both hands.

I had never heard a person's head fracture before. It sounded like nothing more than a deep thud. I remembered everything from the quick pumps of adrenaline through my veins to Paul's face when he realised what I was about to do. It was a mixture of surprise and rage. After the bat connected with his temple, I looked over at my mother whose eyes were pasted with desolation and emptiness. I jumped over and checked her pulse but there was no sign of life. A fountain of tears erupted from my eyes and panic surged through the numbness. Everything I grasped onto was suddenly taken away by one selfish man. I wanted to scream but there was no release from the abyss of my stomach instead, I paced over Paul resisting the temptation to beat his lifeless body into a pulp. While my eyes analysed his frame, I noticed that there was nothing but a small smudge of blood on his head which I thought was bizarre, as a pool of crimson fluid had slowly spilt towards the edge of the room. I walked around his body being careful not to get any blood on myself. My eyes grew wide when I saw that the blood was from his stomach.

I searched the room and noticed the broken bottle in the corner with its spiky edges painted with blood. The answer beamed onto me; it was mother's doing. She had enough of his abuse, so she put an end to it. The panic and sadness inside me subsided, and an instant feeling of satisfaction radiated through me; knowing that my mother had the time to do what she needed and with my help, the prick painfully received what he deserved. Then, a wave of confidence washed over me. I knew that I needed to think through the situation before the police were called. I needed to protect myself. I took the bat to the bathroom and made sure that the traces of blood and my prints were washed off. Being careful, I wiped the bat dry with a paper towel under my hands. I paced to the bedroom and placed it in Paul's gym bag under my mother's bed. Keeping an eye on the clock, I gave myself five more minutes to toss everything in a black bin bag, saturated the content with the leftover stew and rice from the pan. I wrapped the bag inside the old bin bag I was supposed to put outside that afternoon, opened the door to check nobody could see me in the corridor and dropped the bag down the shoot. I walked to the kitchen sink, washed my hands, treaded to the bedroom applied lavender scented lotion and called the police. It took ten minutes for the police to knock the door and by then the tears had fallen, and my face was puffy. I tried to keep it together however, nothing could negate the fact that she was dead, and I was alone. There were five officers and one was a woman who sat with me on my bed in a bid to comfort and soothe me. The male officers walked around the house, urgently took pictures and recorded information. Through my throbbing headache and dry throat, I knew that I had to keep my head straight. When asked, I recited exactly what I saw.

"Okay, Paul, who is your mother's boyfriend, hit her? Is this what you're saying?" I nodded through the tears.

"I went to bed early cause, I wasn't feeling well, and I heard a loud noise that woke me up, I thought someone broke a plate, so I sat on the bed when I realised, they were arguing again." I continued sobbing.

"Then I heard a scream, so I peeked through the door and I saw him choking mum I tried to get him to stop but I couldn't, so I went in my bedroom to look for my phone. Everything was happening so fast, I panicked. When the operator answered, they had both stopped and there was blood on the floor, it was horrible."

The officer bought my story and instructed me to pack a few essentials. I thought they would put me up in a B&B but since I was legally a minor, they found me a foster home. I slowly peeled myself off the bed and threw everything I considered 'essentials' in my suitcase. Phone charger, phone, clothes, body lotion and hair products. I didn't pay attention to where she said the couple lived but I assumed it was somewhere near. Thirty minutes later I was in a car staring at the outside of my home through black tinted windows. Unfortunately for me, my new temporary residence was in Salisbury. I went in for further questioning and I had never felt so alone. The case was later closed however, I grew to realise that even though I had a lucky escape, Paul's family or friends could possibly raise enough suspicions to prompt the police to reopen the case and call me in for further investigation.

I checked to make sure that Andrew was still asleep before I looked through his phone for more incriminating evidence that could potentially ruin my life. I watched the video again and rewind the questions in my head. Did he know me before we met? How did he manage to film it and who else was in on it? I poured the remaining rum in the sink and rinsed out the bottle, glasses and ice bucket that was now a soupy mess. Then I searched his pockets for the house keys and made my way to the fifth floor. Since it was a little after 2 a.m. I walked carefully as not to wake up the neighbours and cause suspicion. Fortunately for me, the stairs didn't have any cameras and the acoustics made it easier to hear oncoming footsteps that would prompt me to hide. As I let myself into Andrew's apartment I was once again in awe with his décor. Without allowing myself to be distracted, I glided between rooms firstly searching for his laptop and secondly, for anything that stood out for motive. I stopped for a moment and wondered how my life had spiralled so quickly but quickly realised that this was the life I had always lived. It was random, full of danger, uncertainty and laughter. The laptop wasn't difficult to find although I couldn't see anything else that hooked my thirst to know more. I grabbed the laptop and went home.

The one thing I enjoyed about staying up late was the stillness of the night. The time when anxieties of the day dissolved into nothingness. I checked on Andrew one more time and as expected he was still asleep. I opened his laptop and tried different password combinations to no avail. I sat back for a moment and searched my brain for more ideas. Then, I consulted the notebook and rapidly flicked through the pages trying different names until one worked: Juliana. When the desktop loaded, I looked through his search history that was empty. Fortunately, I knew how to look for erased files even weeks after it had been deleted. I was pleasantly stunned to see that Andrew had catalogued pictures of his presumed ex-girlfriends indulging in severe sexual fantasies. Not knowing if I would have the chance to access the laptop again, I rapidly plugged in my USB stick and copied everything I deemed relevant. Noting the time, I paced around the house showered and brushed my hair. It was just after 3 a.m. In the corner of my living room, I had Andrew strapped to the chair with a gag in his mouth. Under a normal circumstance, I would have thought it a fitting scene. I patiently waited out the next hour resisting the urge to stroke his arms as he stirred himself awake.

"Morning sugar" I smiled through his confusion.

It took a while for him to realise what had happened and I revelled in the silence as he searched the room for answers. Then his eyes grew wide with the awareness that he was in fact still in my living room, tied to a chair with a gag in his mouth. For a short moment, the look in his eyes confirmed what I thought his reaction would be, to kill me. He was a completely different person to the man I was obsessed with a mere few hours ago. His futile attempt to struggle his way out of the chair was comical. I remained seated with my eyes fixed on him.

"Are you finished?" My face threatened to break into laughter. "Okay babe, I'll remove your gag if you promise to behave. Will you behave Andrew?" He gave a defeated nod. I decided to trust in his promise and removed the gag from his mouth.

"What the fuck is all this?"

"This is me defending myself. Did you really think that you could film me with a client then blackmail me in my own apartment? Or perhaps you thought that you could sleep with me then blackmail me as you did with your ex-girlfriends?" I certainly had his attention now. I wasn't exactly sure if he did blackmail his ex-girlfriends, but his expression confirmed that I was close to his treasured secrets. He suddenly aged a few years as the shock of my words resonated with him, and even with his body erect, I knew just how the roles had reversed.

"What do you want?" I realised that I hadn't always known what I wanted. Since the night I spent with Andrew, I thought of solving the notebook mystery as a fun game. At the very least, I expected a mild exchange of 'no hard feelings' for successfully solving the mystery and now I found myself frozen into the loop of my wants and needs. Since my relationship with him took a left turn, I felt amused and driven in the rush of mischief. Things had escalated quickly, with many questions orbiting my brain. One thing I knew for definite, whatever this thing turned out to be, I wanted to make money.

Andrew and I spent the next few hours together. His lack of participation to divulge information grew increasingly frustrating and I found myself resisting the urge to kill him. I knew that I would hold no leverage on the situation if it confirmed that he wasn't working alone, and I wouldn't know how to proceed with the case. This helped to press the lid on my temper. Andrew was still groggy, cycling in and out of sleep that, of course, pushed me a little closer to my limit. I drew my eyes to the clock, and it was 5.30 a.m. I opened the edge of my curtain and let my eyes absorb the lights over the city. As the minutes went by, I heard the neighbours waking up, TVs and radios being turned on to lift grogginess and accompany their morning routines. Despite my growing predicament I decided to let Andrew sleep while I cooked breakfast and read my book.

Chapter Six

Fuck! The entire time I thought Andrew was asleep, it turned out he was not breathing. It was almost 8 a.m. and I grew tired of waiting, so I let the icy water from my glass of morning smoothie drip onto his face in a bid to pull him out of unconsciousness. I hadn't noticed that the bastard had stopped breathing and for a moment I wished that I had deliberately killed him my way, in a theatrical manner. I realised that the events which lead to the circumstance were mostly my fault for mixing potent drugs with his rum. It had elevated my mood and lowered my inhibitions on a few occasions however, I knew my body and my limits. I paced around the living room for a few minutes trying to think of what I would tell the police. Every step I took pulled a deep pulsing sensation on my temples. The last thing I wanted to do was call the police and answer questions that I didn't quite know the answers to. I especially didn't want files opened to track my record and potentially send me to prison. So, I messaged the one person who had a better idea of how to handle such a situation.

I know it's really early, come to the apartment now. Emergency.

On my way.

I had always admired how keen and prompt Frank was in an emergency. He arrived at my apartment precisely thirty minutes later wearing an overpriced tracksuit. There was no need for us to exchange words, he looked at the rigid man in the corner of my living room and simply exhaled a breath of apprehension.

"It's sort of what it looks like with a hint of complexity" I protested through clenched teeth.

We steeped in a moment of silence. Frank and I had a special relationship. He was my best friend, yet I always felt like I couldn't trust him, until now. Or at least I wanted to trust in this thought, at that moment. With everything I had been through, I felt the universe decided to hand me this moment as a test of our friendship. I remained still while my eyes searched his face for an answer. We had been friends for the better part of five years, and I hadn't noticed the plainness that lurked underneath the contour of his face. When I thought of my memories of Frank, he was always smirking, yet in this motionless state he had ceased into, his face had nothing to give away. No blemish, wrinkles or pimples. I kept my focus on the lifeless body in the corner of my living room situated in the heart of London, the most-watched city in the world. Frank walked to the kitchen, opened a bottle of Patron and took a shot.

"I'll pay the guys to get rid of this, but we need to talk." His voice was toneless, and I didn't like it.

I remained quiet while Frank made a phone call and within ten minutes five young-looking men arrived at the apartment. They weren't dressed out of the ordinary although I knew they weren't the type of city chappies I wanted to have a disagreement or conduct business with. Removing Andrew from the apartment was quick and fuss-free for them with no explanation needed, a better service than most removal van companies. They wrapped his body that was still tied to my beloved chair in plastic and a large cardboard box which arrived flat, then folded into shape around his frame. The neighbours would've thought it was nothing more than a large readymade coffee table in transit. I wanted to raise the question of Andrew's final resting place, but I thought it was best to detach.

After we were certain they had left without a trace Frank took another shot and walked to the living room. I followed close behind with my mind silently judging his early morning drinking.

"Now is not the time to judge love. Removing dead bodies on a Sunday morning is not part of my job or friendship objectives."

"I'm sorry." I bit my lip.

Frank gave me a look I hadn't seen before. It was confusion and anger, he always looked like he had his shit together. Even in that situation, he made a quick decision to get rid of Andrew with help from 'the guys' whom I didn't even know he had. I wasn't quite sure how to digest this shadow of Frank. He took a seat on the sofa and stretched his legs on the coffee table.

"Tell me everything."

I told Frank that Andrew was trying to blackmail me and how things spiralled quickly. I mentioned the video he had recorded, the catalogue on his laptop, the notebook and that I had Andrew's house keys. Frank suggested we perused the apartment again together however, with the building being heavily occupied during the day I recommended we waited until the evening. This gave me enough time to comprehend that Andrew was in fact very dead, and the thought of police enquiries gave me a nauseated feeling in the hollows of my chest. I wondered how long it would take for his friends, family and employer to start enquiring. Nonetheless, I had to come to grips with the realisation that whatever Andrew was doing, he wasn't doing it alone.

◈

Frank

It was the night before Isabella urgently summoned me to assist with Andrew. I finished work and decided to check in on her to see if she wanted to have dinner. It could've been in my head but in between work and my sexual liaisons, I felt a disconnection with her so I thought a good catch up would remedy our bond. Since the last time I had brunch with her, my days had been filled with work, sex and sleep. I picked up the phone while carefully treading my steps to avoid puddles on the pavement.

"Yes?" Her voice seemed urgent which I thought was odd, especially since she never answered the phone in such a manner.

"Well good evening to you too. Fancy having a very late dinner with me?"

"Sorry, can't I'm …busy with something." I decided not to think much of it and expected that perhaps she was busy with her clients. After all, she had to make money.

"Okay, well I'll pop by tomorrow and bring you some breakfast."

She gave me an unsure "sure" and I hurried home. As I walked past the concierge, I noticed a man. My reaction to the presence of this man was the same as someone aware of a ghost in their house. The hairs on the back of my neck stood to attention and a frisson radiated through me. Fucking John. At first, I thought his whining for Isabella was cute, then tolerable and now it was becoming creepy. His hair was sleek with rain and the collar of his shirt crumpled. Despite his wealth, there was something about John that made me feel pity towards him. He was the type of man that made it easy for women to swat him away, and now he was in my building looking solemn like a wet dog.

Since I had a hunch of what the conversation would escalate into, I gave him a nod and invited him upstairs to my apartment for privacy. It was already late, and my stomach was growling. The journey from the ground floor to my apartment was wrapped in uncomfortable silence. Even as I unlocked the door John remained quiet, treading carefully behind me. My ego cartwheeled as I gazed at my newly furnished not so humbled dwelling with pride however, John didn't seem impressed. We walked to the kitchen and I took initiative to pour him a cognac.

"So, why are you here John?" I already knew the answer to this question.

"Let's not dance around the bullshit. You know I really like Isabella. I've wanted her from the first time I saw her. I don't understand…I have everything, and she's still not interested."

"Well, that's Isabella for you. She's a picky bitch." I attempted to lighten the conversation.

"I tried to be a gentleman, and that didn't work so I want to propose something."

Standing still, I sipped my drink and braced myself for the proposition. I'd never thought of this man as a friend but merely someone I occasionally conducted light business with. John was not someone I partied with or told secrets to. The substance of the conversations we had was either about money or Isabella. In fact, this was the first time we had an alcoholic beverage together.

"I have spoken to a few people and I know how Isabella makes money…so I want you to do something for me."

My mouth opened to protest his allegations, but I decided to stay calm and listened intently.

"I want you to get me, Isabella, for one night. I'll give you the money in cash and you can do as you wish with it." I wanted to burst into hysteric laughter though I resisted while his eyes were glued on my face.

"I don't feel comfortable doing that. Why don't you ask her yourself?"

"You can shimmy around the moral samba all you like Frank, but if you don't do this, I'm going to ensure that Isabella and yourself, end up in a thorough interview with the taxman. You may not be selling services on the street corner however, avoiding tax and participating in money laundering wouldn't look good in court, Frank. From my research, I know that you started with providing the clients and she delivered the service, while you both avoided the books. You do know what goes on in prison right? I would ask her myself, but she hasn't returned my calls and well…along with my pride, fancied having myself a bit of fun."

His words stung as they hit my ears. I contemplated calling my guys to take care of him, but people saw us both walking to the apartment, which meant I would be the first to be questioned. Right now, I didn't need the drama. I thought of requesting more time to think about it, but John's demeanour indicated he was not requesting politely.

"People like you think that you can treat others how you please and there won't be repercussions. I'm sick of being swatted away. You have three days. If I don't receive at least a phone call by then, I'm making moves on you both." He finished his drink and threw a small plastic pouch on the countertop near me.

"Five hundred pounds, for the deposit. You have my number" He escorted himself out of the apartment and I held my breath until I heard the door slam shut behind him. I poured myself another drink while contemplating how to approach the subject with Isabella. It wasn't rocket science, I had to tell her. As the cognac smoothed its way through my system, I decided to weigh my options with John's proposal. Then I called the local Italian restaurant for pizza delivery.

Even though the past twelve hours had been an unsolicited trip to hell, I prioritised the need to tell Isabella about John. In hindsight, I'm glad she didn't call to tell me about Andrew while John was in my apartment. She had a lot of experience dealing with men like John and brought some of them to their knees as they swore to stop messing around in hopes that their wives wouldn't find out about their lies. She obviously had a lot on her plate lately so, I drew a deep breath.

"Hey, I have something to tell you." I managed nervously.

"Go ahead."

"John ambushed me in my apartment and demanded a date with you. I told him to leave you alone, but he was quite persistent and-

"I'll do it. Don't worry about that prick" I wasn't sure if she had fully understood what I told her or if she was just grateful for my assistance with the current situation.

"You didn't let me finish. He doesn't want to just go to dinner…"

"Don't worry, I'll make sure he leaves us both alone after the evening ends." She was stern.

Despite her career choice, I knew that she had the mental agility to conduct business, and the deal with John was just that. I really wanted to tell her about the money John had offered however, she had made up her mind and I didn't want to pull away from the real problem which was the Andrew matter. Besides, I didn't ask John for money nor had I spent it, yet. I decided to hold off on telling the entire truth until we made progress with the Andrew mess. We decided to hang tight until 11.30 p.m. assuming this was when time and everyone who occupied the building slowed down.

We passed the time by watching daytime television, ordered takeaways and sipped the occasional whiskey. As much as we wanted to pretend it was a normal day full of anticipated thrills, our nerves had begun to seep through the lid of our valour with uncertainty and questions that mocked our useless attempt to remain calm. Isabella felt the need to shower the day's anxiety off her skin. She extended the offer, which I politely accepted when she was done. In her bathroom, I took the time to lather, scrub, towel dry and when I finished, I borrowed and generously applied her organic coconut body butter that coated every pixel of my skin. I paused to admire how beautiful the bathroom was, especially for its size. It wasn't a sardine tin although it was small, but her minimalistic choice of decor ensured it remained stylish for its compact size. I slid myself back into my luxurious loungewear and prompted our move. We were on our feet sharp at 11.30 p.m. Before we headed for the door, I unlocked my phone to message

John, but I decided there would be plenty of time in the morning to catch up with business administration.

The anxiety crept from the base of my spine to the edge of my temples as we hiked up the stairs to Andrew's apartment. I politely campaigned for the lift however, Isabella pressed that it was safer to use the stairs as residents relied heavily on the lift for impromptu grocery shopping and home visits, whatever the time. We walked hastily down the carpeted corridor keeping our footsteps light to avoid waking the neighbours. Isabella pointed that even though we couldn't hear anyone moving around in their apartments, it didn't mean that there weren't any peeping Toms. We decided that should we get caught, we would pretend to be inspecting the building to update the concierge and make up the rest as we go along. She had smiled when she saw my mouth drop open while admiring the décor in Andrew's apartment. We stood in the corridor for a moment and then decided to check each room.

"Leave everything exactly how we find it." I nodded.

I worked my way through the bathroom checking the cabinets above the sink which contained three boxes of prescription medication including diazepam. I obliged myself to quietly sneak a packet in my pocket and gently closed the cabinet. The kitchen appeared spotless as I carefully checked each drawer while Isabella looked under every cushion, the coffee table and on the bookshelf in the living room. We both froze when the faint sound of footsteps approached the front door. I quietly hurried to look through the peephole while she switched off the lights. We held our breath and relaxed a little when the footsteps disappeared inside the apartment two doors down. It was time to leave. We gave the apartment a final glance ensuring nothing of ours were left behind and silently slipped out towards the stairs back to Isabella's.

She was on the verge of rage as she mumbled that the trip was a waste of time, however, as I felt the bumps of pills in my pocket, I considered it was a small amount of time well invested. It had been a long day and the booze was already out of my system taking my adrenaline along with it, so I looked forward to winding down with a little help from 'Dr Shush'. I almost chuckled to myself reading his name on the label wondering what kind of anxiety Andrew had to make him see someone called Dr Albert Shush. Isabella had started to fidget and pace around the room with her index knuckle on her chin as if she was a university lecturer listening to her students talk shit about ethics. Just as I was about to tell her to stop a muffled vibrating noise came from under her sofa. We both leapt to our knees to find Andrew's phone illuminating in the darkness.

"Don't answer it. I can't believe I overlooked his phone."

The phone stopped ringing and Isabella swiped the screen expecting a prompt for a passcode.

"That's bizarre, he doesn't have a code."

"The creep filmed you meeting with your client from the outside of the apartment then blackmailed you. I don't think he ever let people use his phone or left it lying around."

Swiping through the call log was a breeze as the calls were from two numbers, one called Ryan and the other from his office. Andrew was smart enough to delete his text messages however, he was sloppy with his emails. In the digital age, everyone knew that a passcode was imperative to secure devices. As much as I wanted to play inspector with my best friend, my eyelids were heavy, and I was ready to retire into my divan. I kissed her goodnight and took a taxi home. I arrived home at 1.30 a.m. and by that time the pill I took in Isabella's bathroom had kicked in, I brushed my teeth and slipped under my duvet.

Chapter Seven

Isabella

Life in Salisbury was uneventful. I kept to myself and attended the community college until I turned eighteen. Looking back, I can't say that I hated the place. The day after my eighteenth birthday, I said goodbye to my carers and told them I'll keep in touch. Since I didn't mingle with other teenagers in outings and underage drinking, I managed to save my allowance and asked my carers to open a savings account. When I decided that I wanted to live in London, I purchased a one-way train ticket and booked two weeks in a guest house that gave me enough time to settle and start fresh. My first day in the city was exhilarating and confusing. I ate nothing but a pot of instant noodles and washed it down with a beer. Since I checked in my room early in the afternoon, I decided to explore some local markets and free attractions on the map that clung to my side from the train station.

What I learned from the city was that while the attractions were free, public transport wasn't cheap. With this realisation, I chose to only venture within walking distance from my board. My first night wasn't as quiet as I expected it to be, the constant sirens and the obnoxious drunks kept me awake but I knew that I was where I was supposed to be. My priority was money so that I could find a long-term living arrangement, which meant that I had to acquire a job. I pounded the pavement in the local vicinity with my CV negotiating with cafés and pub owners to recruit me. I wished it was as easy as books and television often portrayed, and it wasn't until 7 p.m. two days later that I allowed my mind and mood to descend into a mini breakdown. It was already day three with no lead on a job and the thought of diving into my minuscule savings just to keep my room was more than I was willing to allow. By day four my enthusiasm to acquire a job had plummeted so I decided to treat myself to a hot drink from the local café. As I walked to the counter a brief panic washed over me as I wondered if the server noticed that something was odd about me. The anxiety eased when I caught a glimpse of myself in the mirror behind the counter, realising that I was only eighteen years old, yet I looked like I had my life together. I placed myself in the far corner by the window where I permitted my mind to slip outside of my reality.

"Are you finished with this?" A deep voice snapped me back to the room. As I looked up in confusion he gestured at the empty mug on the table. "Would you like another one?" He smiled.

"Yes, finished. No thanks, I can't afford another one" I grabbed my bag and made my way past him for the door.

"Wait! You forgot your scarf".

I hurried back to the man and grabbed my scarf. He told me his name was Tom, throughout our conversation I told him that I had been in the city for almost a week and I was broke. He offered me a job as a kitchen assistant. I didn't like the job, but I had a great amount of respect and appreciation for Tom. Not only did he give me my first job, but he also provided guidance.

Chapter Eight

I can't remember what time I fell asleep but woke up with a sore neck and cramps in my right hand from clutching the phone tight during the night. My clock silently screamed 10 a.m. and it felt like it had been a long time since I slept properly. I checked my phone and there was nothing out of the ordinary. Two messages from my clients confirming their meetings and one from Frank enquiring about the date with John. I turned my attention to my stomach, rummaged the kitchen for an easy breakfast and made a cup of mint tea to prep and soothe my stomach. While I sat in my usual spot to gather my thoughts, Andrew's phone rang again, with the screen flashing Ryan's name. My eyes grew with excitement when the idea hit me. Frank would be intrigued by the plan.

After I agreed on a timeframe for my date with John, I told Frank about the plan that my mind conjured over breakfast. Since we had the notion that Andrew was not working alone, I guessed that one of the two recent contacts on his phone was bound to be his helper. I copied The Office number on a webpage to find that it was an IT company in Canary Wharf. I dialled Ryan's number from my phone making sure to block the caller ID. I wanted to have a sense of his manner. I pretended to be a telesales person keeping the conversation light and feeling my ego boost by my ability to improvise without flinching.

"So, the plan is infiltration. I will send a text from Andrew's phone to meet at a café. Of course, he doesn't know that Andrew is gone and I'm the last person he's expecting to meet so there are no suspicions." The words rolled off my tongue like a rotisserie.

"And what about when you show up instead of Andrew, will you say oh hi, I drugged your friend Andrew and now he's dead?" Frank had a point.

"Well, I'll get there before him, pretend I'm a customer minding my own business then wait before he leaves and ask him out to dinner. It's still early, I'm arranging for just after lunchtime so be ready to hang around the usual café for 2 p.m.".

Frank wasn't thrilled about the idea of meeting up with Ryan, but he agreed to support me. I sent the text from Andrew's phone and received a prompt reply. Since the meeting was at 2 p.m. I thought it would be better if I arrived thirty minutes before to avoid looking suspicious. It was still early, so I plugged the phone to my charger in the bedroom, ensured the front door was locked and ran myself a bath. As the salt seeped into my pores and worked its magic on my nervous system, my mind turned to John. His face and memories of our date were now ancient to me however, I felt delighted to know that I made an impression on him. Even though I knew Frank had already agreed with him, I sent a message to John confirming date night over the weekend praying that he would wait until then and refused the urge to harass Frank. It had been a while since I went on a dinner date, so I mentally planned my outfit knowing that as much as I needed to detach and play the game so that he left Frank alone, I still wanted to have a good time and enjoy the sparkle. I made sure to stuff my face with a burger and chips after my bath and poured my body into a leather mini skirt and blouse. I anticipated we would end up drinking at some point during the day so lining my stomach beforehand was wise. I aimed to get Ryan somewhere private. I decided to give Frank a call before I left the apartment, and nothing had changed in his attitude towards the Andrew situation.

"Izzy, when you get a chance, send me the video Andrew had so that I can analyse for clues. If he was doing whatever it is with Ryan and recorded you, they are twisted so be careful."

I bluffed through my reassurance while I took a final glance at myself in the corridor mirror and made my way out.

I sat in the café for twenty minutes nursing a cup of tea out of a mug that needed a thorough scrub when I heard a familiar voice order coffee and toast at the counter. His voice was smooth it was impossible not to turn and look. My eyes followed him as he placed himself in the corner away from the window.

He's here. Quite sexy x

Be careful. x

He slowly sipped his coffee and ate his toast while occasionally checking his phone with his eyes pinned on the door every time it opened. Fifteen minutes later he gathered his phone and jacket ready to leave so I decided to make my move. I caught up with him just as he got to the door and pretended to bump into him. His blue eyes clung to mine while I subtly twirled a strand of my hair and smirked.

"Sorry." We danced around the palpable awkwardness for a moment before I decided to make my way to the door again.

"No, I'm sorry, I was distracted by your beauty." I wondered if he was aware of how cheesy he sounded. I deliberately muttered a 'thanks' and pretended to humble myself.

"Would you like to grab a drink sometimes?" Got him!

I innocently told him that my friend cancelled and that I was free right now if he wanted to. We exchanged our names and confirmed he was Ryan. Unlike Andrew, he wore slim fit jeans and a basic shirt. He had a couple of days' worth of stubbles and smelled like a man who liked to get his hands dirty. I could smell his woody cologne from a mile away but somehow the scent was much sweeter the closer I got to him. His nails were clean, and his hair was short and neat. We walked into a bar across the road and as we ordered our drinks, I could barely recall my behaviour on the way there. Even though I convinced myself that I was in control of the situation, my stomach collapsed into a slush every time he looked at me. A slight anxiety crept through when it occurred to me that he didn't ask whether he met or had seen me somewhere. It meant that he hadn't seen the video, didn't recognise me or just didn't want to let on that he did. I snapped myself out of the trance and asked to be excused while I went to the toilet. I took the opportunity to let Frank know where we were, reapplied my lipstick and walked back to the bar with my game face on. He didn't display any form of agitation or overexcitement but merely a cool calm and collected demeanour. I sipped my bourbon and suppressed myself to his level of engagement while Frank arrived and placed himself at the corner of the bar, just in time to start the game. Ryan pressed his eyes into mine and we smiled.

We were only in the bar for an hour when he asked if I wanted to go somewhere else for a drink and early dinner. The creeping shadow of anxiety in my stomach nudged my mind to politely decline while the adrenaline and my racing pulse were keen to explore the outcome if I accepted the offer. He still didn't let on if he knew me and I did the best I could to act normal. Poor Frank was stuck nursing his second drink pretending to be engrossed on his phone.

"How about we have a drink and dinner at your house?" It was a bold and risky suggestion to make but, judging by the flirting and intense eye gazing I was nearly sure that he was interested in more than dinner.

"Actually, my apartment is only twenty minutes away if you're really up for that?" He smirked. I again excused myself for the bathroom and messaged Frank.

Going to have drinks and dinner at his apartment. 20mins from here.

I noticed a slight jitter in my thumbs as I typed.

ARE YOU CRAZY?! I don't like this

Relux I know what I'm doing. And he's hot! Call you when I get home.

I felt a pang of guilt for dismissing Frank especially since he chose to support me with this Andrew matter, however, regardless of my impromptu attraction for the man, I still pledged to acquire information from Ryan. I walked back to the bar prompting our exit. I took an opportunity to search the bar for Frank but was disappointed to see he had already left.

◇

Nothing much was said on the way to his house, I quickly noted that his taste in interior décor was much different from Andrew's. His apartment was bare and exhibited basic furniture and white walls, a minimalist of sorts. The air was lighter and the sunbeams from the giant windows lured me into a state of relaxation.

"Not what you expected?" He asked as he made his way across the open plan living room to the kitchen.

"No, I mean I don't really know what I expected. It's lovely though" I said as I planted myself in the armchair.

He returned to the living room with a bottle of whiskey, two glasses and a takeaway menu.

"Do you need a mixer?"

"Nope" I grinned.

I browsed the food menu as he poured the drinks scrunching my face at the dishes it offered.

"Don't you like Chinese food?"

"Nope, how about we order pizza instead?"

I expected some form of objection, but he remained calm and agreed. We ordered from a local restaurant using an app delivery service which indicated a thirty-five minutes wait. It was plenty of time for me to work my magic. We sipped our drinks and engaged in basic chatter about anything and everything but ourselves. I excused myself for the bathroom and checked my messages. Surprisingly, there were no concerned emojis from Frank. I suppressed my guilt by imagining he was somewhere living it up in a club. As I made my return to the living room my phone vibrated indicating our food was just down the road. The doorbell rang as soon as I sat down this time, picking the space a closer to Ryan. He opened the door, exchanged words with the delivery man and we got stuck into our meal.

"I'm glad you're not shy to eat in front of me" I raised an eyebrow mid-chew.

"So, do you work close by?" I decided it was time to get the ball rolling.

"I work in Waterloo for a finance firm, how about you?" This was the test.

"I'm a freelancer…I have a successful blog on interior design." This wasn't a complete lie. At first, I created the blog as a hobby but then as my content grew, so did my audience.

"Cool, well I'm glad I bumped into you today my day was going to be quite dull."

"Really? How come?"

"I was supposed to meet my brother for brunch, but he ditched me. He's probably hungover with some bird in his bed". I suddenly fell in a coughing fit and the floor started to float underneath me.

Out of concern, he reached over to check if I was alright but I pretended to have nearly choked on a piece of dough, yet, all I wanted to do was grab my bag, a slice of pizza with a swig of whiskey and be on my way. Ryan didn't let on that he knew anything of me since we met, and I started to wonder whether I wasted my time and energy on the wrong person. Regardless of who he was threatening or not, I needed to find out who Andrew was working with and why I was a prime target for his game. I decided not to waste more time and politely excused myself to leave.

"What's wrong? I thought we were having a good time."

"Yes, and now I want to leave. So please excuse me."

"It was your choice to come here." He exhaled and followed me to the door. Yes, it was my choice to go to his apartment. When I was so sure that he had something to do with the fuckery that my life had become and now, I wasn't sure. Just as my hand touched the handle on the door, he placed his warm hand on my neck and my knees nearly buckled to the floor. He leaned closer to me and let his breath glide into my ear.

"I don't want you to go" I had heard those words many times from men. The type of men who were willing to throw their last cents and overdraw their bank accounts in exchange for one more night. This time, the words caught me by surprise and really made me want to stay. His lips lightly traced the side of my neck while his hands made their way to my hips.

"If you're not leaving, you should close the door." His whiskey tainted voice commanded.

Relenting to his instruction, I gently pushed the door closed and removed my hand from the handle. I turned my face to the side encouraging his lips to find mine, and when they did, I felt something that I hadn't felt in a long time. I felt like myself. I turned around, placed both hands on his face and drew our kiss deeper while we glided across the living room and fell on the sofa. With my eyes shut, my mind focused on the intensity of the kiss while my hands rubbed and felt up every inch of his muscles. Every time our tongues intertwined, I wanted more. Our breath thickened with each other's scent. I positioned myself on top of him. His hands softly grabbed and pinched my skin. Our mouths remained glued on each other's faces and neck while I grinded on him feeling his manhood rise. He wanted me and I was happy to oblige. His muscular arms enveloped me into his warm chest as I slowly opened his trousers. He let me go long enough to manoeuvre my skirt and knickers. I reached in my bag and pulled out a condom which he tore open with his teeth. Within a second his hands were sliding across my breasts as he slid into me. The intensity of our energies pulled me into a trance and all I could focus on was his body. We kissed each other hard the whole time my hips swirled as I relished him. Just as I was about done, I couldn't resist digging my nails into his shoulders. Nothing about this was right since I slept with his brother, drugged him and got rid of his body. Nonetheless, at that moment it felt like a distant memory. My mind snapped back to him as a ferocious groan escaped from the back of his throat. I sunk my teeth into his neck, and we remained still for a moment before my skin began to prickle with embarrassment, I excused myself and headed for the bathroom. When I returned, he was sitting on the sofa with his jeans pulled up sipping his drink and without giving the atmosphere a chance to settle into awkwardness, I took the glass from his hand, shot the rest of the spirit and smiled like the professional I was.

"Wow."

"I know. I'll see you around." I made my exit without giving him a chance to lure me into a state of emotive delusion. I got a cab home and my chest collapsed with a breath of relief as soon as the door slammed shut on my back. The entire apartment looked gloomy with nothing but a faint glow from the sunset peeking through the ripples of the curtain. It wasn't until I switched on the lights that I noticed the clock presented its numerals on the wall. I was caught in his spell and lost track of time. I checked my phone to find a message from Frank but decided to call him instead.

"Really bitch, you couldn't drop me a text sooner? I've been anxious all day."

"You're such a baby" I chuckled through the phone.

"Look I'm sorry for ditching you, I do feel bad about it, but something happened and I'm not sure about this anymore." I bit my lip.

"Fucking hell, did he hurt you?"

"No, but he said he was in the café waiting for his brother so obviously his brother is Andrew. Hello?"

A slight pause lingered on the line. "You can't trust him then."

"Well, I slept with him". It felt natural to say it out loud.

I didn't have the chance to explain the motive behind sleeping with Ryan as Frank's mouth was grating out a million profanities. After a very long rant about using our heads, not thinking with our hearts and genitals he managed to ground himself and asked for the details.

"Well, at least you didn't ditch me for slob. I also managed to watch that video and it looks like the person recorded it from the building opposite yours. With a very expensive camera."

"That's freaky, I no longer care how they did it I just want to know who else was in on it and why."

"And we will. I'm going home now, been on shenanigans since this afternoon and my head hurts."

After I got off the phone with Frank, I paced my way to the bathroom where I dumped my clothes in the laundry basket and immersed my body under the steaming hot shower. As the beads of water swept the lather away, I allowed myself to think about the events of the day. I thought about his firm hands stroking my body, his soft lips brushing against mine and how unyielding my desire was for him. I moisturised my body, pulled my curls in a bun and looked through Andrew's phone from emails, apps to search history. Again, there was nothing I hadn't seen before. As I safely tucked the phone in a box on the shelf my phone beeped.

Date with John definitely on for Saturday.

A few hours ago, I didn't mind going on a date with John one more time however, with Ryan's scent still clinging onto my skin I thought it was a massive burden.

Frank and I didn't see each other for the rest of the week and If I was honest with myself, it was a pleasant relief. I thoroughly enjoyed spending time with him although I wasn't looking forward to exposing every detail of my time spent with Ryan. As much as I wanted to bathe in the memory for a while, every passing hour felt like a noose tightening around my neck. Before I had a chance to dig deeper into the Andrew situation Saturday arrived, and it was time for my date with John. Since I hadn't seen Frank for a few days, I thought it was appropriate to invite him over. Despite my need to keep some detail to myself, it was a ritual of ours to drink wine and gossip while I got ready to go on a date. It had been a while since we did this, so I bought him a small bag of party pills as a gift. The temptation to take one myself grew with each passing minute however, I decided to stick with brandy instead. Frank, on the other hand, had pupils the size of the good fortune cat parked on the counter of the local Chinese takeaway.

"I feel good!" He giggled while his head bobbed to my playlist. I took a shot of my drink and poured myself another one. I shimmied into lace underwear just as fast as I shimmied out of my leather lined outerwear.

"I want to look incredible, but I don't want him to think that it's all for him," I said while I rummaged through my wardrobe.

The date wasn't until 7 p.m. so we had time to dance around, drink and eat the snacks Frank brought. We eventually decided to stick to a simple lace dress and heels for the drama. At 6 p.m. Frank and I parted ways while I took a cab to meet John on the west side of the city. The traffic wasn't too bad although, I cursed the driver for avoiding the main roads and tricky junctions. John had conveniently chosen to have dinner at a hotel in Chelsea where he booked a room for the night. Upon arrival, the host led me to the restaurant. As we weaved our way past tables and sophisticated chatter, I scanned the restaurant for recognition of my many clients. Fortunately for me, there was only one man in that restaurant who knew about me. As we approached his table John stood to greet me and exchanged polite words with the host. The scent of soapy liquid on his suit immediately offended my nostrils but, the multiple shots of brandy I had with Frank removed the spiky edges from any form of awkwardness that slowly lurked in the atmosphere.

"You look beautiful as always. How have you been?" I didn't know whether I wanted to laugh or snarl at his phoney attempt of conversation.

"I've been fine just trying to live my life." Throughout dinner, he dragged the conversation about how much money he was making, spending and lending which prompted me to wonder whether I should make more of an effort to recruit him onto my list of clients.

Besides the fact that his hurt puppy attitude increasingly repulsed me, I thought that since he had been obsessing over me for a while, he would be glad to have any type of relationship if I presented him some attention. As we nibbled our way through the main course, I took opportunities to lightly touch his hand and gaze into his eyes with the ambition to bring home an envelope full of cash or a cheque. Surprised by my display of affection he leaned closer to me and asked if I wanted to go up to his room for a drink. He paid the bill and we made our way to his room which was a family-sized suite with an impressive view of the city. John didn't waste any time making his move. He leaned in and kissed me as soon as we walked in the lounge and I didn't hesitate to kiss him back. The kiss was pleasant, and it reminded me of our first date although now the stakes were high, I wanted him on my list and off Frank's back. We kissed for several minutes and all along I was wondering when he would peel off my clothes. Boredom began to consume me. Despite the slight fumbling around, he managed to take my clothes off without assistance. As we rolled around on the bed my mind flashed back to the many liaisons I encountered with my clients and I began to rate them all on a scale of one to ten. John's schoolboy skills were somewhere around five since he didn't have the same confidence in seducing me as he did, dealing with money. With the humorous image dancing in my head, I pulled him on top of me while I exaggerated an over the top moan of pleasure that encouraged him to finish quickly.

"That was nice." He said as he breathed into my neck. I lightly kissed his cheek and moved from underneath him and scurried to the bathroom. I took the opportunity to shower and walked back into the bedroom wrapped in a luxury bathrobe.

"You're leaving?" I took this as my queue to perform my sales pitch.

"Not at all. Why?" I coyly asked.

"Well this is just nice, I…"

"Look I like you but let's face it we're two different people, I'm not relationship material and you only care about money." This was concrete in truth. I had seen some women over the years and wondered why they subjected themselves to such humiliation. Always wanting and needing love from a man who chased the things that would always be most important to him. The job and the money. Before my father died, I used to look at my parents and told myself that this is what life was about. I dreamed of meeting someone who would make me feel incredible, get married and have kids, but now that I was older and wiser, I thought it was possibly the worst mistake a woman could ever make. Ultimately, the only person who could make a woman feel strong and incredible was herself.

"It could become an arrangement if you were interested…" His head shot back to me quicker than a bunny binkying from excitement. He was so close to the edge of the hole that a whiff of wind would've pushed him straight inside. My ego began to gloat, and my lips curved into a subtle smirk.

"Maybe in the far future, but I already gave Frank the payment for tonight." My heart leapt into a bowl full of rage as the words stung my ears. I wanted to break open a pillow and fill his mouth with cotton. I was angry at Frank for not telling me and even more so as I watched the bastard gaze nonchalantly outside the window. How dared he? I gathered my thoughts and simmered my temper down to the charming personality I had played all evening.

"Oh?" I said with exaggerated confusion.

"Didn't he tell you? I thought you were best friends. Five hundred pounds it was." This was nowhere near my usual price, I was offended.

"I'm sure he had an explanation but why did you do it?" The rage was rising and this time I didn't want to control it.

"Well I didn't think you would come otherwise. You haven't returned my calls."

"You're such a fucking loser. I would've respected you more if you asked and paid me upfront instead of demanding under the counter like a silly schoolboy." My insults snapped him out of his gloat and his cheeks grew red with a combination of anger and mortification. I paced around the room to get dressed, put on my shoes, grabbed my handbag and headed for the door.

"Prick!" I shouted as the door slammed shut. As the lift slowly glided from the suite to the ground floor, I took the time to steady my breath and tidied my hair. I knew that I overreacted, he had already initiated the game with Frank so of course, he would've dangled his wallet to win although, I had to admit it still stung that Frank didn't tell me about the money. I marched to the hotel reception and asked the handsome receptionist to direct me towards the bathroom and to my relief, it was discreetly tucked away in a corner behind some vintage screens. I quickened my walk to a cubicle and delved into my bag checking for my belongings, cards in my purse, my housekeys and most importantly for John's wallet that I swept into my bag when he distracted himself with the city views. The compartments were bulging with cash and all sorts of credit cards which I didn't see the point in keeping. I transferred the money to the bottom of my bag, flushed the toilet and walked to the sink. I didn't hear the cleaner walk in as she surprised me with her serious demeanour. She scanned my frame, her eyes remained glued to my shoes. I walked closer to her and handed her two fifty-pound notes with the wallet.

"Could you do me a favour and leave this under a table in the restaurant, please?" I kept my eyes focused on her and she gave me a playful smirk.

"I like your shoes." I fished my hand into the bag and gave her another fifty-pound note.

As I made my way out of the door, I heard her whistle and mutter a few words. I walked towards the tube station and hailed a taxi. At home, I spilt the contents of my bag on the bed and counted the notes which totalled eight hundred and fifty pounds. The money wasn't more than I would've earned with a client however, it was certainly enough for a night out. I was satiated knowing John would be thoroughly inconvenienced when he realised his wallet was missing. I messaged Frank for his location, he pinched back the address of a club not too far from his apartment.

I checked the time and noted 1 a.m., it was still the weekend and I needed to blow off steam.

Chapter Nine

Frank

Isabella arrived at ROUGE a little after 1:30 a.m. and I immediately noticed her irritation. A slight panic rushed through me with an image of John's body lying cold somewhere under Chelsea bridge. I trotted to her with a wide grin, but she grabbed my arm and dragged me to the women's toilet.

"I want my money. John told me he paid you for my service." Her brown eyes burned into my soul as she stood with her arms crossed.

"Fuck, I tried to tell you in your apartment after Andrew, but you didn't let me finish."

"I don't care. Give me my money." She slammed her bag on the sink and I flinched. I'd seen her angry before however, it had never been towards me.

Isabella always kept her emotions under the surface in confrontational situations, it was a part of her charm, she never allowed herself to lose control in public. That night though, John must have really gotten under her skin.

"Fine, I'll transfer it to you via the app right now. Look I tried to tell but I should've tried harder. My bad." I opened the banking app on my phone, transferred five hundred pounds and waited for her to confirm receipt. She nodded her head and I saw her mood ease.

"Let me buy you a drink and if you still hate me after that I'll leave you alone." she agreed, and we walked back towards the bar. Just after I ordered our drinks my phone buzzed with a message from John.

I'm not satisfied. A weekend break is due I'll come by Monday morning.

My heart pounded in my throat and a feeling of doom slithered around my neck. I thought about paying the guys to deal with John however, too many people had seen us together recently and I couldn't kill someone every time they inconvenienced my life. Besides, I didn't want Isabella to sink deeper into this mess. I drained my drink in one go and ordered another. The more I blissfully drank my way into a blackout the better the music at *ROUGE* sounded. I grabbed Isabella's hands and we danced into the early hours of dawn.

The midday sunlight announced itself through the curtain. My mouth was dryer than a desert, my head was overflowing with fragmented faces and regret from the night before. I planned to blow off steam while Isabella entertained John but then he flipped the coin and I lost control. As I lifted my head off the pillow to navigate my eyes around the room, I felt a sense of doom realising that I wasn't in bed alone. The giant bump under the duvet stirred. The duvet lifted and there he was all chiselled and smooth, in my bed. My mind froze as I searched my memory for the timeframe of our rendezvous to no avail. Then I realised that I had an unknown naked man in my bed, and I felt like a tramp. He stood out of bed and I noticed that he was wearing underwear which I knew for sure wasn't mine. I remained glued to the mattress while my eyes searched for my phone that was on the chest of drawers across the room.

"Don't worry we didn't fuck. And I'm not a thief either." He threw the phone and I caught it with my shaking hands.

The unknown man made his way to the bathroom and left the door open. I checked for messages as soon as the steamy melody of the shower slid into the bedroom. There was only one message from Isabella confirming she arrived home safe at around 5 a.m. So, I sent her a reply announcing the weird treasure I uncovered and scrolled through my photo gallery in a search for answers. The recent photos like my memory was a mixture of black smudges and blurry shapes. The hacking headache forced a jolt through my spine forcing me to lock my phone and gulp two prescription-strength painkillers.

"You okay Frank?" I wasn't quite sure how to answer such a question.

"Who are you?"

"Oh" He looked stunned and defeated. "I'm Mathew, we met a few hours ago you were shitfaced and said I could crash here."

"Erm, I doubt I voluntarily told you to crash here." I spat back.

"Technically no you didn't, but you could barely walk I found you leaning against the sink in the toilet."

"Toilet?"

"Yeah at *ROUGE*. I tried to get you into a cab, but the guy wasn't having it. So, I got in with you. You were a mess." Confirmed, I was a tramp.

I slowly sunk into my hole of shame while Mathew made coffee and served scrambled eggs on toast which I could barely keep down. After an hour of silent chewing and awkward glances, I had a shower and simultaneously fired questions at Mathew about the night before. He told me we met in the club's toilet and that I kept mumbling things about money and called him John which he thought was my boyfriend. I asked about Isabella and he claimed she got into the cab behind ours. I received the text message from Isabella reassuring she was fine, so I wasn't worried for now however, doom crawled over me as I remembered John's message. Suddenly, everything flushed back, and I saw it all clearly. He wasn't satisfied with the date and wanted to go on vacation with Isabella. The solution was simple I knew that I had to tell her. The entire situation was nothing but a fluff of mess, the man had become obsessed with her and I began to fear for her wellbeing. I couldn't tell the police since John had some dirt on us and even if he didn't, he had enough connections to ensure we got into trouble for something. He was that petty. I stood in the shower with the water beating into my pores and considered calling the guys to handle the situation but after Andrew, I grew weary of becoming too messy. Just as I snapped myself back to the room, Mathew announced that it was time for him to leave. We exchanged phone numbers and decided to meet up sometime during the week. Even if he was beautiful to look at, I promised myself to never lose control again and to never take random strangers back to my apartment. I spent the rest of the morning nursing myself back to health keeping my mind sharp for my meeting with John.

I had cursed Monday multiple times in my life however, anticipating John's presence in my apartment made me really hate Monday mornings. The doorbell rung at 10 a.m. and I gathered my thoughts while John ascended. His mouth curved into a grin and it took all of my energy to not punch his teeth out of his mouth. I had no problem with wealthy men who had to swing their ball sacks around to get ahead in the world. They usually did it to make up for shortcomings in other aspects of their lives. I knew that I had done my fair share of ball swinging in my time however, I didn't have the audacity to barge into someone's apartment to blackmail them at 10 a.m. on a Monday. Especially not sporting a grin that could potentially provoke someone into beating him to a pulp.

"Don't you have to work?" He was trying me.

"I should ask you the same thing." We froze into the tenseness and glared at each other.

"So, the date was fun, did she tell you about it? I felt that it was a bit rushed though, so I want to take her away for a while. I have to travel to Cumbria for work soon."

"There's something wrong with your head mate. You came here before to harassed me, I got you what you wanted and now you want more? Fuck off!" The man was really getting under my skin.

"You do realise what would happen if you don't set this up right? She actually proposed I became one of her clients, so I have the leverage to end both of you." He giggled to himself.

I couldn't believe Isabella would be so silly to engage with this creep. Yes, he had the money but it sure wasn't enough to deal with this bullshit. I felt sorry for his parents and his friends then I realised that they were probably demons just like him. I thought within the situation I didn't have a choice but to agree, and I would work out a plan with Isabella later.

"It's settled then, I will contact you with the details soon." I waited for him to leave before I sent her a text.

John just left. He wants more. Need to sort this out asap call me later.

Don't worry. We've got this.

I gathered my bag and made my way to work, the place where I could escape for a few hours.

Chapter Ten

I cringed every time my mind flashed back to my behaviour back at club *ROUGE*. Poor Frank looked stunned when I lashed out over a few notes. He had seen me angry before although, I told myself I would never do that to him. In the early days, our friendship was nothing more than alcohol-infused laughter, parties and culture. Since the Andrew situation happened, our friendship had unexpectedly elevated to a level of trust that I didn't want to jeopardise, and I certainly didn't want to lose my temper over five hundred pounds which either of us could earn in one hour. I took a moment to wonder whether John realised that his wallet was missing and thought nothing else of it since he got what he deserved for being a prick. He was an even bigger one for pushing Frank over the edge. Something jerked in my stomach when I received the message and somehow, I had a feeling that John would've never left us alone, so I thought it was time to play the game and win.

Since I didn't have any bookings for a couple of days, I thought a spa day would contribute positively towards my mental wellbeing. The thought of Ryan had slipped my mind and the memory of Andrew simmered into a distant image hung on the furthest wall in a foreign art gallery. I showered, dressed, pulled my hair in a messy bun and made my way to the five-star hotel which was located just twenty minutes from my apartment. I thought about ordering a cab however, the sun was finally shining so I decided to walk along the river with my eyes absorbing characters by the shop front while my camera captured the talented artists showcasing their work on the pavement. Upon my arrival at the hotel, I was greeted by a cheery receptionist with turquoise eyes and bubble-gum pink lipstick who instructed the policies and escorted me to the changing rooms. I sported my tribal two-piece bikini and positioned myself in the corner of the sauna. There was only one other person in there, so I took the time to look around and let my mind focus on the present. The man sitting on the other side clearly felt uncomfortable with my presence and decided to leave five minutes after I sat down. It had been a while since I pampered myself and I refused to let anyone steal my focus. I laid on the bench for fifteen minutes when the sauna door opened, and a beautiful woman walked in. She smiled and planted herself on the bench next to me. While we seeped in humid silence, I wondered what she did for a living, wondering if she was as powerful in her profession as her presence here next to me.

"Do you do this often then?" I wasn't keen on sauna small talk, but I felt obligated to indulge her.

"Not really. I never really have the time. Do you?"

"Maybe twice a month when life gets stressful."

"Well, I know all about stress. Most of it is from men." She agreed and we both giggled. We fell into silence again. Then it occurred to me that a stranger was fishing conversation from me. I grew wary of this woman with each passing minute, so I battled with myself, and tried to disengage. It would have been good measure to leave however, I was enjoying the sauna and her company.

"I haven't heard from one of the most stressful ones in a while so I'm celebrating…"

"Oh yeah?" I prompted her to continue.

"We were together, you know the usual, then shit happened, and he just wouldn't leave me alone. Haven't heard from him in about a month." We both giggled. "It's for the best".

"I'm Izzy." It occurred to me that we hadn't introduced ourselves and I gave her my nickname just in case she decided to google me.

"I'm Juliana." My mind flashed back to where I'd seen or heard of that name before. Then I realised it was from Andrew's notebook. Questions and scenarios played out in my mind. I seized the opportunity to enquire further.

"Nice to meet you. Maybe we should grab lunch and a drink when we're done here." I tested my luck. She nodded and agreed. If she was from the notebook, I wanted to know all about her and potentially the kind of relationship she had with Andrew. Though, chances were that this coincidence was all in my head.

After two hours of pool dipping and a deep tissue massage, I met Juliana in the changing rooms, and we decided to have lunch at the hotel's restaurant. We parked ourselves at a table with a view by the bar and the waiter promptly arrived to take the drinks order. Juliana ordered a white wine and I fluttered my eyelashes as I asked for a whisky. Impressed with my choice of beverage, the waiter winked and proceeded to the bar. We engaged in small talk about the weather until the drinks arrived and I took the opportunity to try something out of the ordinary from the menu, tuna tartare with a side of carb. Juliana opted for a grilled salmon and salad, a dish I grew tired of cooking. The food arrived quickly, and we devoured every morsel with minimal conversation. Since it was a weekday the restaurant wasn't busy, and the waiters showered us with attention.

"So, what do you do for work Izzy?" I thought about telling her the truth but then I remembered that I wasn't stupid and gave her the usual answer.

"I'm a blogger." She looked unimpressed. "I have a background in curating art for small galleries. I became tired of working on a routine, so I applied my expertise to social media working with artists and interior designers remotely." She loosened with relief.

"Sounds amazing and challenging. I started my company two years ago it was a rollercoaster ride but worth it." We clinked our glasses in pride. "It was so good back then. I was single and carefree until I met a man."

"That's usually the case." I smiled.

"At first the dating was fun but when I told him I wanted nothing more he became a bit obsessive." I remained silent while my interest was drawn into her story. "He would send me flowers and call me five times a day, so I told him to leave me alone or I'd call the police. He broke my kitchen window."

"Wow, he sounds like a piece of work. Did you call the police?"

"Yes, but they didn't have any evidence apart from the missed calls which were somewhat strategic. So, when he came knocking at my door drunk one evening, I took selfies of his hands around my neck. He must've been high too since he blacked out. The next day I showed him the pictures and threatened that if he didn't stop harassing me, I would show the police." The wine worked its magic as she poured another glass along with her life story.

"Did he stop?"

"No, so I did it. I was desperate and scared for my safety. I had an accident at the gym a week one afternoon, so I walked into the station with it and showed them the pictures. I told them he was so drunk and kept telling me to take the pictures then he'll let me breathe like it was some sick foreplay. They believed me and arrested him at work on the same day." I became even more impressed with this woman.

"I'm not judging you. You did what was necessary for your safety."

"I didn't press charges though. I just wanted him to see how far he pushed me. He still called me after that reminding me of how angry and hurt, he was but, he knew better than to continue with the harassment. Sometimes he would send a drunken angry text, but I filed it and then ignored him. I haven't heard from him in about a month."

My heart gravitated towards this woman as she took matters into her own hands to protect herself. Part of me felt that she was a better woman than I could ever be, if my feet walked in her shoes, I would've sorted him out with one of my special cocktails. In this case, I already did even though it was accidental nonetheless, he was still dead.

"Anyway, I knew he was seeing other women after me since he always complained about them on his drunken calls and texts, I know it's terrible but as long as he wasn't bothering me, I really didn't care and wanted to move on with my life." Brutal honesty, I liked it.

"I hope I never meet him." We both giggled.

"Just don't date anyone named Andrew." I nearly choked on my drink as she spat the particles of his name in my ear canals. I wasn't sure if it was the same person but, I didn't think it was a coincidence that her name was in his notebook and his name just slid out of her stories and onto the table. Being aware that she could probably sense something was wrong I kept my composure and resisted the urge to ask further questions. I also realised that we had been in the restaurant for nearly three hours and I wanted to keep a clear head while I digested all the information at home. We exchanged phone numbers and I reassured Juliana that everything would be okay and to call me if she needed anything. I wasn't sure where this newfound relationship would go but I was hoping to gain more information about Andrew's demons.

After my departure, I decided to walk back along the river in a bid to clear my head and try to process everything I absorbed within the last few hours. It was rush hour, the city chappies in suits and female tiger sharks in pencil skirts with their feet gripped in designer heels emerged from their matchbox offices, marching to the pub or the train station. Their sour faces relaxed with relief as the buildings slowly faded in the background, I felt reassured with the professional decision I made to not sign myself into a typical office job years ago. As I made my journey along the river, I avoided cyclists and runners deployed in sync on the pavement, with great efforts to avoid bumping into pedestrians. The walk seemed to last longer than what I was used to as the whisky sizzled with the afternoon heat that summoned a heavy tingle in my legs. As I walked inside my favourite local restaurant to buy a takeaway dinner, the hairs on the back of my neck stood to attention when I noticed a man I recognised by the counter.

"One salmon portion, veggie dumplings and rice bowl please." He slouched over the counter and swiped his phone. I deliberately stood next to him and ordered my food.

"Well look who's here." A contented smile stretched across his face.

"Hello to you too." We stood and stared at each other in awkward silence.

"We like a lot of the same things. Since you're here we might as well sit down and eat."

I had planned to eat my dinner in its disposable container on my living room floor yet since I was already out and feeling peckish, I accepted the offer. The food took ten minutes to arrive and during that time I checked my phone and twiddled my thumbs while Ryan stared at the characters parading along the river. I took the time to analyse him and took in his rugged yet sophisticated look. He was wearing a plain shirt and slim-fit trousers though I doubted he had been to work. His jaw was covered in stubbles and his hair looked slightly dishevelled. My stomach fell into a pit, digesting the idea that it was possible he spent the night in another woman's bed. I kept my breath under control and focussed on satiating my growing hunger.

"So, Ryan." I paused, realising that I had never uttered his name in a proper conversation and wondered if he preferred Ryan or something else.

"Ryan is fine." He smiled.

It also occurred to me that we hadn't seen each other in nearly two weeks. I snapped my mind off the ludicrous assumptions and negative thoughts at the same time the server brought our food to the table. As I tucked into my dumplings, I realised that my jitters and tingles had subsided. Ryan had no problem inhaling his salmon as we sat in the silence that sizzled our auras. The shop was quiet and the only sound that echoed through the room were the slurps of our green tea and the chomps of our jaws. We finished our food and once again seeped into the awkward silence. (I was growing sick of the awkward silence). I tried to think of a subject for conversation however, nothing came to mind. How could this be? To be honest, I wasn't sure where I emotionally stood with this man and I certainly didn't want to overcomplicate the situation since I also slept and (accidentally) killed his brother. Which prompted a reminder to fish for a conversation on the type of relationship they had.

"Are you ready for round two?" His words snapped me back to the table. I wanted to smack him across the face with my purse, scoop my food containers and run.

Yes, I engineered our meeting, seduced him and he probably saw me as nothing more than a pretty face with a plump peachy arse, conversely, a deep part of my being felt a connection with this man. I had a small hope that he would've felt the same or at least be willing to comprehend that it could have been an opportunity for something good. On the other hand, I allowed my emotions to fight with logic and wondered where exactly I expected this thing to go.

"I'm joking Izzy." Goosebumps rippled through my skin as I observed his automated addressing of 'Izzy'.

"Do you prefer to be called Isabella instead?"

"Isabella is the name I gave you isn't it? I suppose Izzy is fine." He looked somewhat shaken out of his comfort zone and I rather enjoyed seeing him fidget through the discomfort.

"I have some things I need to prepare for work so I'm sorry I can't stay." I narrowed my eyes to the floor to shield my disappointment.

"Cool."

"I can't remember if I gave you my number but here it is. I would like to take you on a proper date. Call or text me your availability." A warm smile stretched across his face.

"Sure."

He shoved his phone in his pocket and left the shop while his aftershave lingered in the air. If he had asked me out on a date a week or even during the first few minutes of our meeting in the restaurant, I would've leapt at the invitation with excitement, but after I analysed the energy between us something felt off and he seemed distracted.

By the time I arrived home a heaviness decanted on my shoulders and I felt dizzy with anxiety. It had been a few weeks since the Andrew situation and the days of fearing the police or unknown associations knocking my door at ludicrous hours were long gone. I managed to keep up appearance and lived life without breaking a sweat. Even after I showered the heaviness remained, this time it had accumulated into a fog that made me question the choices I had made in my life. I decided to fight my way out of the negative self-indulgence by doing something I hadn't done in a long time. I lit a candle, sprayed some lavender sage and meditated for an hour. When my eyes finally opened, I knew exactly what needed to be done. It was time to soldier through the way I always had.

It was just after 9 p.m. so I decided to invite Frank over for a chat. While I awaited his arrival, I checked Andrew's phone for absent new emails and texts messages which I thought of as odd since it looked like he used the phone for work. It was odd that no one had pestered him or even called to check that he was okay. Then I recalled the conversation I had with Juliana and second-guessed if the Andrew she had trouble with, was the same Andrew who had tried to fuck up my life. I decided to call his office's number pretending to have missed a scheduled meeting. To the receptionist's surprised, as far as she was concerned Andrew had not worked at the firm for six months. I continued to ponder on the situation. The doorbell snapped me out of my thoughts.

"I should look into cutting you a key. Come in."

Frank bounced inside the apartment wearing super skinny jeans and a basic designer shirt which suited him very well. At first, I grew slightly anxious that he would've kept a grudge following my behaviour at the club however, his cheery attitude showed that he had other positive things occupying his life. I found this trait of Frank endearing. Our friendship had shifted into new territory, one of trust. I would always remember what he had done for me. The day I messaged him to help me with Andrew, I knew that regardless of what we did and didn't tell each other, that he was loyal. He bounced to my side in my hour of need with minimal fuss and for that, I would always be grateful to him.

"You really should but then I'll be here all the time."

We engaged in mundane chatter as I made some tea, exchanged the usual compliments, complained about the weather and gossiped about our neighbours. We then quickly moved on to more serious matters. I told Frank about the phone call to Andrew's office and he wasn't shocked.

"He probably got sacked for gross misconduct. Dipping his pen in company ink or something." We pondered in silence for a few seconds. "Try not to get worked up we'll get to the bottom of it. I think you should be more careful with your clients especially new ones. Maybe book appointments at a hotel."

Frank proceeded to elaborate further into his not so much of a one night's stand with the gorgeous man from club *ROUGE*, Mathew. His face scrunched into an exaggerated expression at the horror of waking up to a stranger in his bed and even worse according to Frank, willingly inviting a stranger from the club to crash at his apartment. I couldn't help but fall into fits of laughter while I tried to reassure him that it wasn't the worse thing he had done.

"Remember when you asked me to pretend to be your fiancée to get your inheritance?" We both ceased and rolled back in laughter and agreed that it certainly was one of the most absurd things he had done.

Driving all the way to Yorkshire to visit his grandmother who greeted us with a bitter smile and cigarette fumes, instructing us of the rules, regulations and family traditions before he could receive his inheritance. "You need to ensure she's a right fit my dear" I heard her press on the subject while I busied myself making tea in the kitchen. Frank remained tight-lipped about his sexual preference even when we were squished together on a tiny divan in his childhood bedroom. Giggling and joking about how much easier life would be if he was into women.

"I'm glad you accept me for who I am." He kissed my forehead. At that time, we had nothing to reveal about ourselves, yet we had shared a lot of information about each other, disguised in cryptic and hypothetical circumstances. It wasn't until the final day of our visit that dear old grandma revealed that she knew of Frank's trickery and his agenda after browsing and clicking a few social media pages and expressed her disappointment in us for deceiving a senior family member. "I still have a few years to get that mean old bitch!" He had said every so often. I wanted to enquire if it hadn't occurred to him to approach the situation with authenticity and perhaps charm the lady with his fabulous personality and warmth, of course, I then realised that authenticity hardly got anyone anywhere.

As we sipped our teas, a low vibrating sound came from the corner of the sofa where Andrew's phone was on charge. We rushed to the phone while the screen lit to indicate a missed call. I wasn't sure what I expected. A text message from Juliana and Ryan or even a voicemail from his parents. Although I must admit that I hadn't given any thoughts about Andrew's parents but since they hadn't contacted him, I assumed they also must have thought of him to be a menace. Either that or they were dead. As I swiped the screen there was no name assigned to the number on the missed call. I shrugged it off as a sales call, but Frank made an interesting point that they rarely called from a mobile number. We redialled the number and blocked Andrew's caller ID. The call rang three times while we held our breath for the mystery caller to answer.

"Hello…hello?" Frank and I glared at each other in disbelief as I ended the call.

"That sounded like him. What is going on?"

"No, it can't be. It's like impossible, hold on." Frank typed the number into his own phone and pressed the call button then hung up before the line connected. Sure enough, John's name flashed on the screen.

I had no idea that Andrew and John had any kind of relationship, but I could understand why they would be suited for a friendship since they were both dicks with money. My mind started to spin, and I realised that it was possible John worked with Andrew to blackmail me. Frank progressed to express John's second demand for a weekend getaway that I didn't hesitate to agree to. My only condition was for Frank to demand more money that we would share before my departure. Of course, I expected John to remain on his toes which was fine as ultimately, I was going to beat him at his own game. In hindsight, this was all stupid and childish. If John felt I had disrespected him in some way by rejecting his date invitations or whatsoever, he should've approached me instead. I concluded that perhaps he felt easier it done through Frank since they had interacted frequently through their financial dealings and cordial greetings. Perhaps he anticipated Frank to be the weaker one to buckle under pressure. Frank and I giggled as we continued to conjure more plans of extortion. Since John wanted to continue the games, Frank and I were stronger if we worked and played together. We decided against any communication with John through Andrew's phone and thought it was best that the entire subject was left alone for a while. It was possible that they only met to talk about money and plan their next blackmail. I knew deep down that they were both involved in illegal activities. Frank left shortly after he messaged John to confirm my agreement for the short vacation. I wasn't ecstatic about the situation especially upon the new discovery however, it was a pivot in a lead that I accepted would increase the chance of me getting to the bottom of the slippery mess that had become my life.

Life was quiet when I settled into my job at the café. I lived in my board for two more weeks then moved into a studio across the road from the café were Tom helped me with all the necessities. I was a sceptic of his generosity, wary that he would worm his way into my bed however, I learned that Tom was just a man with an honest heart. His wife died in a car accident three years prior and he didn't have children. I met his sisters who frequently covered shifts in the café and his mother who supervised the menu. As I grew into the woman I was destined to be, and I also grew into a support system that helped me settle into my new life. I never called my foster parents because I wanted to forget everything about Dorset. I didn't have any friends either, therefore, starting a new life wasn't difficult.

I started to frequent the local gym to train my body and mind and ultimately, to meet new friends. It went well at first, I realised that I enjoyed Pilates. It wasn't until the third session that I was called out in front of the entire class for 'stealing' a woman's spot in the studio. As far as I was concerned, all spaces were first come first served. She made a show of calling me out which left me flustered and full of self-doubt. I contemplated leaving although I realised that I had paid for the course upfront, and I was doing myself no favours by running away. I swallowed my pride, apologised and continued the class. The next session I arrived extra early to ensure that I was the only person in the studio. I saw that the mat was already laid out for queenie, so I placed a bottle of water next to it, providing extra customer service. I left the studio and lingered in the changing rooms making myself late for class. When I walked in, she had already sipped a quarter of the water, rolling her eyes and hissing through her teeth as I walked by. I placed my mat in the back of the room and proceeded with the routine while occasionally noticing that Miss Whiskers was looking a little loose as she flowed through her poses...perhaps a little too loose. It only took fifteen minutes for the elixir to work and watching her tumble to the ground was as satisfying as watching people cut soap on social media. The class halted and the paramedics were called. Later, it turned out that Queen Bee was a frequent drug user and had overdosed on a mixture of Adderall and Vicodin that gave her a heart attack. Her death was reported to be an accident as she had a history of prescription drug abuse and fortunately for me, there was only one camera in the studio which pointed at the receptionist.

I could say that I felt bad about the situation and that I never meant for her to die but that would be wrong. I saw the world as natural selection just like in the wild, you either ate or you got eaten. Queenie was satiated. She became entitled, lazy and expected people to roll over every time she spat at them and I wasn't one of those people. I wanted to make something of myself, I was full of anger, and that drove me to do the things I did. I had a vision of what I wanted my life to be and refused to let anyone make me feel inferior. I continued my sessions for the month then I decided to go to the club with my new friends. I met a few good-looking men and learned how to deal with one night stands the same way every grown-up did. The walk of shame. I had discovered my love for bourbon and sex. I realised that I enjoyed the solitary life and all I had to do was remain prepared for anything and everything. The need for control was embedded in my core and I felt confidently grown-up. I eventually found a new job working in a bar that turned out to be an underground sex club where the rich mingled in private. Tom was disappointed to see me leave however, I remained a part of the family for the following year before they closed the business and moved to Cyprus. Admittedly I felt sad, though ultimately, I knew it was time to move on. He slid an envelope through my letterbox when I was at work that contained one thousand pounds in cash and a note.

'Isabella, it had been a pleasure. Remember everything we taught you and stay out of trouble. Stay streetwise. From all of us-Tom.'

The money remained in my savings account and grew with interest. I knew they would've been proud. Working at the club paid well and I met a lot of interesting people.

It had been a week since Frank and I discovered that John had a connection with Andrew. Even though we decided to leave the subject alone for a while, giving us time to process our next move, I was anxious to find out what type of rapport Andrew and John had. We arrived at the hotel in the Lake District and although John was the last person I wanted to be there with, I had to admit that it was a much-needed break from the city. Checking into our room was a breeze and I was pleasantly surprised to walk into a suite with floor to ceiling windows showcasing Lake Windemere's breath-taking beauty. Even more of a surprise, the suite had two bedrooms located on both ends of the corridor.

"I thought you might prefer your privacy". John uttered from the bar. Words couldn't describe how much I despised the man, yet it was in that moment that I thought I saw a glimpse of humanity in him. Or perhaps he wanted to lure me into a false sense of security. I managed a faint smile.

"I have a couple of people I have to meet before dinner. Business and all that." His posture remained taught.

"Okay, what do I do in the meantime?"

"Order whatever you want or try the spa. It's up to you." His face unreadable, he fiddled with his bag and handed me a copy of the room key. He poured himself a stiff drink and made his way out the door.

My shoulders collapsed upon his departure and I waited a few minutes before quickly working through his bags. I had no idea what I was looking for but, I thought anything of relevance would lead me one step closer to the truth. I checked the bags, patting my way through jackets and trouser pockets to find nothing but toiletries and an old restaurant receipt. Of course, it did occur to me that John was not a stupid man who would leave anything of importance in his bags with an escort who successfully robbed his wallet. I quickly washed my hands and made my way to the spa. I was greeted by a cheerful receptionist who instructed me of procedures and left me to my own devices. Luckily, the spa was empty as I made my way through the changing room.

He's at lunch with douche friends. In the spa.

I messaged Frank.

Lucky you. Enjoy while you can and stay diligent.

As much as I wanted to enjoy my time there, I knew that it was going to be a challenge to survive three days with John knowing that there was a possibility that he was the one working with Andrew to record the video. My ego was bruised over the fact that Andrew played me. Here I was, engineering a love game between us, only to find out that he had an agenda to ruin my life. The only question that nagged at me and made the back of my neck itch was *why*. I had never met the man in my life and somehow, he knew things about me that only Frank did. At first, I explored the reasoning that it could've been Frank, but after everything we had been through and how he had my back the day he found Andrew's rigid body in my living room, I knew better. So here I was at a spa in Cumbria. Despite my predicament I thought there would be no point wasting my energy on thoughts about things I had no control over. The worse outcome for this situation would be that I ended up in prison or dead. I shrugged the robe off my body and slid into the jacuzzi. I lingered on the edge of anxiety for a while, but I soon settled into the low hum of the jets and allowed my body to sink into the soothing chaos of bubbles around me. My heart halted as my thoughts were interrupted by the beautiful man rinsing himself under the shower by the pool. Of all places, I didn't expect to bump into him and yet here we were in Cumbria oblivious of each other's burdens. His eyes widened as he turned to walk towards the jacuzzi.

"Well, what a pleasant surprise." I was indeed surprised, though I wasn't sure if it was pleasant or inconvenient.

"I would say the same, how are you, Ryan?"

"Better now that I know you're here. It's a bit far from London isn't it?" He plotted himself in front of me and leaned his back against the jets.

"I'm here with a friend, fancied a change of scenery." It wasn't a complete lie. I needed the change of scenery although I would have preferred to be there with Frank.

"Ah! I'm here with a friend too, he's here on business and I had some free time, so I took the invitation as an opportunity to let my hair down." He smirked.

We seeped in silence for a moment which was nothing new to me. I was amazed that we shared our most intimate breaths and sounds a few weeks ago in his apartment, yet every casual setting we reclined into, we had nothing of relevance to talk about. I took this moment to analyse him. Tracing my eyes on his hair studying the faint lines on his forehead and every strand of an eyelash that fringed his blue eyes. His neck textured with veins and every inch of his body roped in muscles. I hadn't thought about his relationship with Andrew, and a silent twitch of guilt pinched my stomach although seeing him laidback in the jacuzzi, I wondered that perhaps they were not close but merely two men who met up with each other from time to time because they were obligated as brothers. If that wasn't the case, then maybe he didn't know that his brother was dead.

"You don't hold back do you?" His words caught me off guard and I widened my eyes in confusion.

"You were staring at me. I'd like to know what's going on in that head of yours."

"Nothing and everything." I kept a straight face. He moved closer to me and my body squirmed as his warmth prickled my skin.

"A woman of mystery." His shoulder and arm were now touching mine. Alert of my acknowledgement, he turned his body to face me and we stared into each other's eyes for a moment. I would've enjoyed this moment more if I wasn't aware that we were half-naked in a jacuzzi with the possibility of John walking in. Just as my mind started to spin from the heat that rose from the bubbles and Ryan's body, he kissed me hard and bit my lip. We kissed for a moment while his hands rested on my neck, hesitant of where this would go. I pulled back and attempted to detach myself from him.

"Don't go."

"I don't understand what you want from me." I snapped.

"I told you to call me but you didn't so I should ask you that same question." The truth was that I didn't know what I wanted from this man. My life was messy and unpredictable, the last thing I wanted was to fall deeper into shit that would distract me from the answers I was trying to find. I did know for sure, I liked kissing him. I liked the way his hands slowly caressed my lower back as his lips traced my neck. He grabbed my hand without a word, and we walked towards the changing rooms.

"We don't have to do this. I just want to get to know you. I'm in room 206 and have nothing planned for the rest of the day so give me a knock if you want to do something." I gave him a sincere nod and made my way into the ladies changing room.

Ten minutes later I was pacing around the suite like a child high on sugar. I hadn't been high in a while and quite frankly I didn't miss it. Kissing Ryan felt like I had been introduced to a new drug. My body reacted to him in a way it hadn't with other men. Just as I sunk deeper into my thoughts, John walked in. I couldn't tell if he was in a good mood or not, something was off. His eyes were lazy, and his pupils dilated black.

"Are you alright?" He walked over to the sofa and kicked off his shoes.

"Fine, just signed a good deal. Not after a drinking challenge though." I was taken aback since I never knew John drank like that. I knew him as the man who sipped pinot noir and read broadsheets, not the type who shot tequila and sucked kegs but then again, I supposed we all had to do things to get ahead in life.

"Have you eaten?"

"No, I just got back from the spa."

"I already ate, sort yourself out." I had no problem doing that. I went through the food menu and nothing tickled my fancy. When I looked over at the sofa John was blissfully echoing his snores around the room. I looked at the clock and a slight irritation crept through me as it was only 6 p.m. I grew frustrated at the uncertainty of this situation. I tried to depict his game. I wanted to fuck him and get this vacation over with. I walked over and gently patted him awake, fortunately, he had slipped into dreamland. I grabbed my bag and made my way to room 206. The door opened immediately after the second knock and my heart fluttered at the warm grin that greeted me.

Frank

For all the drama she and I had been through lately, I was glad that Isabella could get away from the city to clear her head even if it meant being in Cumbria with John. Isabella had dealt with a few dick lords since I met her, and I had no doubt that she could handle John. I was excited to hear about her meeting with Ryan and even though she said dinner was nothing more than casual conversation and mild flirting, I suspected that something immensely romantic was yet to develop between them. If she had not accidentally killed his brother and looped me in the mess to get rid of his body, it would've been the perfect fairy tale. I hadn't thought about our lives beyond partying, popping pills and sipping wine but lately, I started to wonder if this was it for us. She was certainly not parent or marriage material which worked out fine since she didn't want children and I deemed the only thing worth spending my credit card on, were ourselves. Marriage and kids were definitely off our table. A message from Mathew, did I fancy lunch? I was mildly excited at the prospect of lunch.

Sure

I fired back with a smirk. My memory was still fragmented from that night at *ROUGE*, I still refused to believe that I invited a stranger back to my apartment to spend the night. It was even more difficult to believe that I slept in the same bed as him and didn't have sex with him. I really hated John for messing with me. I was no saint, but, I had never blackmailed anyone under the influence of desperation. I hadn't heard from Sebastian in a while either. I missed the time I would have a few sick days off work, and we would stay in bed all day, drinking prosecco ordering junk and fucking until one of us tapped out. We had a no strings attached relationship therefore, I wasn't concerned that he went off the grid. That was his personality, he had a need to be alone sometimes and I never protested. It allowed me to pursue other ventures. At 2 p.m. I was worked up an appetite for lunch. Since I was already dressed, I messaged Mathew to meet me at the apartment and thought we would walk to the café together. He arrived twenty minutes later, and I was ecstatic to note that he had swagger just like me. We didn't have much conversation over lunch, the awkwardness was palpable, so I jumped in the driver's seat and took the wheel.

"What have you been up to since the last time I saw you?"

"Nothing much, work. You?"

"Same." It wasn't a lie. I kept myself busy while Isabella was away and savoured the peace of mind that John managed to ruin when he started blackmailing me.

We sat in silence once more before I thought it would be a good idea to invite him back to my apartment so we could break the ice over a bottle of whiskey but then the waitress arrived with our food. I wasn't feeling particularly hungry nonetheless, I sipped my soup to ride through the awkwardness.

"Look, this is a bit weird…I haven't seen you in ages and you weren't pleased to see me in your apartment after *ROUGE*. I just want us to get to know each other."

We starred at each other then I got him to engage in the usual 'tell me about yourself' scenario. His story wasn't all that special. He grew up in London, loved his job and didn't have any children. We ate and sipped our way through the minutes until I decided it was time for us to leave. Mathew offered to walk me home however, I sensed that perhaps he was interested in hanging at my apartment for a little longer. We barely made it through the front door before his hands made their way down the front of my trousers. The thud of the door slamming shut behind us disintegrated effortlessly as our lips leeched on one another. No words were needed. With my back taught against the wall, he made his way to peel down my trousers and boxers. I wasn't nervous nor did I expect him to follow through, yet he did. His eyelashes fluttered as he eagerly worked on me. It had been a while since I got intimate with someone and the built-up energy was ready for release. My body tensed as his mouth worked its magic to bring me to the brink. A short moment after, he stood up and traced his thumb on my mouth, smiled and walked to my bathroom. I collapsed onto the bed, as my heart pump adrenaline into my spine. I wanted more. He made his way to the bed, kissed me and reassured that we would meet again. Then he left. At that moment, I considered that maybe this man was someone the universe had in line for me but then I sighed at the realisation that a long-term relationship was never written in the stars. I knew that I could never part with my ego. The satisfaction I got from men chasing me was something I couldn't let go of.

Isabella

John had lingered around the suite really early in the morning and I pretended to mind my own business while eavesdropping on his business calls and peeking over his shoulder at his screens. I was sitting on edge as I waited for him to demand sex or have his colleagues walk in to kill me. Truth be told, I thought about slipping something in his drink to end this mess quicker. Taking him in as he paraded around, brewed nausea and thirst I hadn't satiated in a while. I wanted to kick his head through a mirror. I distanced myself by thinking about dinner with Ryan, that developed into a pleasant evening. We talked about blogging and giggled over the most ridiculous things we'd heard people say in the city. It was effortless and the chemistry consumed me. I wondered about the company he kept that brought him to Cumbria however, I couldn't go digging out his life if I didn't want him in my business.

"Is that a smile?" His voice snapped me back to the room. John stood facing me with a bottle of water snug in his hand. He slowly walked towards me and his hot breath coated my cheek as he leaned closer, eyes admiring my frame.

I knew he needed control, so I let him lead. His hands, now free, unbuttoned my top to reveal my lace bra. I slid my way up the sofa and felt the diazepam I took in the bathroom creep into my blood. He climbed on top of me, unzipped his trousers and traced himself on my mouth. I felt nothing as I humoured him with a grin and a light moan. His eyes, dark with entitlement and lustful expectations. I slowly teased him. His body tensed. My lips parted and he slipped inside, releasing a grunt of satisfaction. I used my hands to end it faster and allowed him to glide deeper until it was done. He climbed off me, zipped up his trousers and announced he was going to a meeting and wouldn't be back until dinner time. In the bathroom, I brushed my teeth, gargled mouthwash and soaked in the shower until my core turned red with heat. The high had subsided, and I wanted more. I needed a release. Getting dressed was effortless as I only exhibited my lingerie and a trench coat. Yes, it wasn't original and yes, I knew that men loved it. I grabbed my bag and made my way to Ryan's room. I had a lot of nerve to do this, it was history repeating itself. I just prayed that I didn't bump into him in the lift. I approached the door with caution, in case John was lurking somewhere and eventually gave a slight knock. He was wrapped in a towel with droplets of water slithering down his body. Muscles taut, and hair glistened. I made my way to the sofa and loosened my coat. Cliché. His towel dropped to the floor revealing every inch of him, a masterpiece. The world stopped for a moment and when I caught my breath, we were on the floor with his eyes pierced through mine.

"Not now, not like this Isabella. I've wanted to do this again since the moment we had dinner but you're hiding something. I don't need to know what it is, but you can't hide behind intimacy."

I didn't feel embarrassed or frustrated. His words pinched my heart. A million thoughts raced through my mind and one feeling was in my heart. In this insanity, I was falling for him.

As I sat at the coffee table and picked at my pancakes, my mind swirled back to Ryan. Just as I finished, the phone rang.

"Hi Sexy." Ryan's voice sounded calm and refreshed. I couldn't help but smile.

"Thank you for being a gentleman earlier. Fancy lunch?" It dawned on me that my feelings were growing more real for this man.

"Sure, be ready for 1 p.m.". I couldn't hide my excitement.

Lunch with Ryan didn't happen, as John instructed that he needed me on his arm for his business meeting with his clients. As they all laughed and sipped their spirits, my mind wandered to a life without crime. I couldn't think of a time where I wasn't so ruthless. Even as a child, though I seemed to have it all, I always had to fight for what I wanted. To make other kids respect me and for teachers to like me. I had to be ruthless, learning in class and on the playground. I also had to be ruthless with Paul. But now, even more so, ruthless with my emotions. I locked them away. I grew irritated as I sat and pretended to engage in conversation with John and his clients. I was losing time and I needed to end this debacle.

"Yes, Isabella here is a blogger".

I didn't spend too long talking about what I did. All they needed to know was that John surrounded himself with creative people with credible reputation and motivation to attract wealth. It also wasn't a bad thing that I had a dazzling smile. We sat at the table for over an hour when I realised the numbness in my backside. I grew restless and John shot spiteful glances as though I was a misbehaving child. Thirty minutes later we departed back to the suite with John's satisfied grin after securing the deal.

"You were nearly going to blow this for me". He spat as we entered our suite.

He paced around as he loosened his tie, unbuttoned his shirt and nagged about how much it would've cost him to lose the deal. He had the contracts signed by three new clients and all he did was linger on the negative. I removed my shoes, walked briskly to my room, changed into a pair of leggings and a simple top. By the time I walked back into the lounge my head was swirling as John carried on nagging. I felt the nausea radiate from my stomach to my throat. I tried to breathe through and push past the haze, but he just would not stop. So, I smacked him on the head with a bottle of gin.

"Now look at what you've done". I muttered as he descended into a blackout.

I stood over him as the haze subsided and the rhythm of my heartbeat echoed in my head. The silence in the room, amplified the humming of the minibar. I looked at John, stretched on the laminated floor. My body, rigid as the coldness crept in through the tip of my toes. Fuck, I lost control. Again! I didn't want to call Frank and drag him deeper into my mess so, I got to work at tying him to a chair the same way I did with Andrew. Except this time, I didn't drug him and would keep him alive until I decided if he was worth this life. One thing was for sure, I was irritated and tired of playing games. It was time to get answers and I was doing it my way. John was heavy to lift and carry but I managed to get him onto the desk chair with a rope wrapped securely around his feet, wrists and waist. This made it easier to wheel him to the bedroom where I untied the rope and tipped him on the bed. Thank goodness I worked out and planned ahead of time to travel with supplies. A slight panic surged through me at the thought that there was an opportunity that he might wake up but fortunately for me, he didn't. I didn't have a plan. I didn't know what questions I wanted to ask or what the hell I was going to do after I got my answers, if I ever did. I attempted to calm my mind for a few minutes as my eyes panned towards the minibar. I couldn't let the volatility of whiskey cloud my judgement. Especially not in the Lake District. I was alone. I reasoned that maybe I should call Frank, but I feared that one more issue would push him over the edge and most importantly I feared being judged for losing control. This was one of the things I never spoke to anyone about. My fear of losing control. Nonetheless, that was the truth. I lost control with Paul, Andrew, Miss Whiskers and now with John.

Chapter Eleven

Isabella

I suppressed the memories of Dorset as I clawed my way through adult life, and even when I was in my highest moments of joy, I had a pinch of uncertainty in my chest. It was a shadow that traced my guilt and twisted it into a rage I tried to control. I did the best I could although people knew how to push my limit. John knew how to push me and this time, I was already falling off the edge. I paced around the suite and traced a mental map out of this mess. Logically, if I got rid of him all of mine and Frank's problems would go away, however, I still didn't know the depth of his game and I wondered if Ryan had a cosy bed made up for himself in this hole. Then, an idea hit me like a sharp punch in the belly. I decided to call Ryan to the suite for a drink. John was out like a log, so I thought the only way to get to the truth was to ask them both at the same time. I laced the whiskey with codeine and had the glasses ready for his company. Five minutes later he was standing at the door with a grin on his face. I invited him in and let him sink comfortably into the sofa. John was tucked up quietly, in his bedroom.

"Thanks for coming." This wasn't a lie. I was happy he showed up.

"Thanks for the invite. Your place is nice."

The least I wanted to do was hurt Ryan, so I poured him a small drink, enough to get him lazy and loopy in case he fought back. He stood up and walked towards me. Twirled a strand of my hair around his finger as his lips brushed against mine. I didn't know what was going to happen in the next hour, so I savoured his kiss.

"I'm so sorry."

Those were the only words I mustered to say. Although there were many things I should've been sorry for, I couldn't think of anything specific. I guess I just felt bad for dragging Ryan into a mess he didn't deserve to be in. I knew something was off when he walked in the room. He seemed nervous. So as soon as the infusion hit his bloodstream, I saw the glint in his eyes fade with confusion. I felt bad for doing this until his phone rang. I answered the call but only listened to the person on the line. I recognised the voice. Julianna. I wanted to cry out of jealousy, scream out of frustration and punch him. His eyes were loopy, and his body was loose, which made it easy to bind his hands and feet with cable ties. I was tempted to force more of the elixir down his throat. I checked on John in the next room and he was still unconscious. However, the bruise on his head was twice the size and there was no way I could let him go back to London after all of this. Moments later Ryan stirred back to consciousness and his eyes grew wide when he realised that he couldn't move.

"It would be in your best interest to calm down," I smirked, of course, I was in no mood to joke around.

I pulled a stool and sat down in front of him. My mouth was moving at Ferrari speed as my brain tried to make sense of the questions I wanted to ask. I told him about Andrew although, I didn't confirm Frank's involvement. I spoke about John's blackmail and his games.

"Then I suspected that maybe you had something to do with it. But after that day in your apartment, I doubted myself. I let my emotions get in the way of my investigations. It was stupid, but I hoped that whatever we had was real. So, tell me why I was chosen for this game?"

We sat in silence for a long time until he began to sober through the confusion. I was on the way to losing patience so I made myself a cup of coffee and a snack.

"It wasn't supposed to be like this."

Involuntary tears cascaded down my face. His voice was deep and soothing, but I still needed to hate him for potentially fucking up my life.

"You need to untie me, and we can forget this ever happened." I remained silent as he pleaded.

"Untie me now Isabella or you end up spending the rest of your life in prison. You need to stop whatever it is you think you were going to do with John. I know he's here."

I untied him and he jumped straight up to find John. I followed close behind and halted when he found John unconscious on the chair.

"Shit!" He spat.

We walked back to the sofa and he kept his eyes on me.

"Who hurt you to mould you into this violent person Isabella?" I remained silent, thinking about my next move.

"I know Juliana through Andrew. They went out for a long time and it was nearly two years ago that she told me what he was like with her. I told her to leave him, but Andrew never took no for an answer. So, I helped her to use the abuse story for the restraining order. Then I found out about the other women he blackmailed out of revenge for what Juliana did to him. He did this to women because he thought it was Juliana's fault that he lost his job. I confronted him, told him to see a therapist but he refused.

Then one night I invited him over for drinks and he brought John. They got so drunk and started talking about their plans and the women they blackmailed. I wanted to find a way to stop him without going to the police because he was my brother but before I had the chance, he had met his match with you. He sent me a message with a picture the week before I met you. He told me who you were and said you were gorgeous. My god, you are gorgeous. We were supposed to meet and when he didn't show, I got worried and called John. John sent me the video that they had of you, and I knew you weren't someone to be caught in the trap. I recognised you when you initiated the first contact with me at the café. I had a friend look you up and nothing appeared. You're invisible. You're not even linked to your own social media account. What are you hiding? Whatever it is, it must be a gruesome part of your life that you're so desperately running away from. We're both chasing breadcrumbs here but it's because of what we have, I'm asking you to stop this."

He held out a hand and beckoned me to him. I really wanted to trust him. I wanted him to mean everything he said but I knew that it was better to detach from other people's words. I offered to make us both some coffee so we could sit down and talk. Ryan was aware I didn't trust him and I'm sure the feeling was mutual even though he may have thought he really wanted us to live through this nightmare together. I knew he was watching me, so I slipped a capsule from my sleeve into his coffee. I stirred the extra hot liquid until the capsule disintegrated and handed him the cup. I took a sip of mine and exhaled my apologies about his brother. He sipped his and nodded to my tears. We sat in silence and looked at each other until his eyes went blank. His body slumped deep into the sofa as his stomach expanded out his last breath. I stood up and took the time to look at my prince. He looked like he knew what was coming and sacrificed himself for me. And I knew that I couldn't stop this once I had started. As much as I thought I was falling for Ryan, I had learned to never trust accomplices. He had the opportunity to stop Andrew, yet he didn't. He didn't try hard enough. I was growing a guilty conscience since this all started but I was delighted to know that I had helped a lot of women by removing Andrew from this world. I made my way to the room where John was leaning towards the light. I had all the answers I needed to move forward. Subconsciously, I knew John wasn't going to make it from the beginning. He was a dick. I left him as he was and pulled an empty syringe and injected air into his vein. It didn't take long for his heart to stop. My phone vibrated; it was Frank. I didn't want to drag him into this, so I rejected the call. I piled the glasses and coffee cups in the dishwater and initiated a thorough wash, wiped down surfaces and grabbed my belongings with my purse and all necessities I came to the hotel with. I considered the cameras around the hotel and thought that when the police called, I would confirm they had an argument and I left. My priority was to get out as fast as I could. Moreover, aside from Ryan and John, nobody knew who I was. John's business associates barely acknowledged my existence at dinner. I did the best I could with the mess and thought that perhaps a lifetime of solitude in prison would be a good outcome if I got caught.

I managed to slip out of the hotel without any suspicions, got myself a cab back to the city. It was expensive but I needed to be in the safety of my apartment, with silence on my side to think about my next move. I called Frank and told him everything. He didn't take the news well, nonetheless he was glad John was off his back without incriminating himself. I vowed to never drag Frank into this regardless of the consequences for I was responsible for the choices I made. I told Frank to go about his daily routines and keep his distance for a while, in case the police were sniffing around.

It had been six weeks since I'd been at home, meditating on my alibi. I gloated in supremacy knowing that I hadn't made it easy for the police to track me down after the incident. I had since changed my hair, started wearing coloured contact lenses and had stopped sourcing new clients. The plan for Frank and I to keep a distance until the dust settled in the press was working. The police had confirmed the incident but had not released in-depth information about the victims. The hotel was prestigious, and I profited from their desire to stay quiet to protect their brand. My nerves relaxed as time passed. I had been anxious to switch on Ryan's and John's phone, for fear that the police could track them, but I was mostly afraid of finding something I didn't want to. So, I woke up with the strength to say no. I had entangled myself in a web of lies and murder, and all I wanted was to live my life as I dreamed. Both phones were switched off, so I wrapped them in an old cloth and threw them in my bag. I left my apartment with caution and I glued my focus on arriving at my destination. I took my usual route along the river, passing shops and cafes. My heartbeat matched my feet as they pressed on the pavement. It was just after the morning commuter rush therefore, the only people around were keen tourists and joggers who were too concerned with keeping their hands warm.

I found a quiet spot in the middle of a bridge and admired the breath-taking view of the city that had since pierced a hole in my heart. I removed the phones from the cloth and tossed them in the water, along with my anxieties. As I stood on the bridge, I watched my breath float into ether and released the tension in my shoulders. I made a decision to live my life as fabulously as I could. To be more careful with clients and to never allow anyone to use me as a pawn in their games. I was ready to live with my mistakes and transmute my experiences into lessons. I smiled at my mental monologue and thought about how lucky I was to get away with so much without even trying very hard. The truth was, I could get caught. I had choices. I could sell up and move abroad, stay in the city and be extra careful or, I could jump in the river to end it all.

END

Printed in Great Britain
by Amazon

31849271R00078